Count I

A Play in Three Acts

by Ted Tiller

Based on Bram Stoker's
Nineteenth Century Novel
Dracula

A SAMUEL FRENCH ACTING EDITION

SAMUEL FRENCH

FOUNDED 1830

New York Hollywood London Toronto

SAMUELFRENCH.COM

COUNT DRACULA, sound tape
❖ ❖

Please be advised that Samuel French, Inc. can furnish a sound effects tape for the above play UPON RECEIPT OF THE FOLLOWING:

1. Name & Address of organization.
2. Exact performance dates.
3. Deposit of $25 (which is refundable when the tape is returned in good condition after performance).
4. Music royalty of $10 each performance.
5. Mailing charge of $3.00.

All monies MUST be sent before tape is shipped to your theatre. Music royalty is not refundable in any case. This tape is rented for 6-8 weeks only. Please order the tape far enough in advance so we can ship it to you on time for production.
Samuel French, Inc. can NOT ship the tape to you for any longer than the 8 week period.

STOCK Royalty terms quoted upon application.

"COUNT DRACULA" was first produced by Stephen E. Hays at Stage West, West Springfield, Mass., on December 10, 1971, directed by John Ulmer, setting by Robert Federico, with William Guild as Stage Manager, and with the following cast:

(In Order of Appearance)

SYBIL SEWARD	*Diane Hill*
HENNESSEY	*Richard Larson*
DR. ARTHUR SEWARD	*John Wardwell*
RENFIELD	*Raymond Singer*
WESLEY	*Glen Lane*
JONATHAN HARKER	*Richmond Hoxie*
MINA	*Hannah Brandon*
COUNT DRACULA	*Eric Tavares*
HEINRICH VAN HELSING	*Jerry Hardin*

SCENE

Living quarters in Dr. Seward's Asylum for the Insane, north of London.

ACT ONE

An autumn evening in the first half of the Twentieth Century.

ACT TWO

Nearly midnight, three nights later.

ACT THREE

SCENE: 1: Twenty-eight hours later, before dawn.

SCENE 2: The Crypt at daybreak.

Count Dracula

ACT ONE

TIME: *An autumn evening in the first half of the Twentieth Century.*

SCENE: *Living quarters in Dr. Seward's Asylum for the Insane, north of London. The room has traces of Fifteenth Century Gothic architecture. Its stone columns and arches evoke a long gone yesterday. It has been modernized for the comparative comforts of the 1930's but it holds a darkness, brooding quality. It is a place where ghosts might walk. For less harrowing purposes it combines living room, library and office for Dr. Seward, his sister and his ward. The room is high above the ground, so high that neither treetop nor housetop is seen through the open French windows Up Center. Only the sky is visible, the horizon broken by Count Dracula's castle on a distant hill, silhouetted in the night with a solitary light burning in its tallest tower.*

There are gauze curtains and heavy, somber draperies at the French windows, each on traveler tracks controlled by drawstrings. Both pairs of curtains apparently are manipulated by actors onstage; then again they open mysteriously on their own— via unseen backstage crew. The French windows themselves open without visible aid at Count Dracula's will. Beyond the French windows a shallow balcony extends past their frames at both sides. The balcony railing is waist high and must be strongly braced for it sees much action, some of it violent. Right of the windows is a fireplace with an impressive mantel and a grate of glowing coals. Over the mantel hangs a large oil portrait of some-body's rather formidable ancestor, circa 1885. The portrait is painted on scrim through which Count Dracula makes a ghostly appearance in Act Two.

There is a fire bench before the hearth and Right of the fireplace stands a tall wooden stool with rungs for Renfield. A triangular bar fits into the Up Left corner of the room. Bar has exposed up-per and lower triangular shelves for glasses, bot-tles, Seltzer water, etc.

Downstage Left a flight of stairs without a hand-rail and with low risers, making it scarcely more than a gradual ramp, leads up to the outer hall and main entrance, to the dining room, Dr. Seward's laboratory, etc. A wide bookcase in the wall of Left stairway, near its lowest steps, is hinged at its Left side to swing open upstage for some of Dracula's nefarious activities. Late in the play the duplicity of this bookcase is discovered and used by Mina.

Down Right a stairway with normal risers, hand-rails at each side and a landing platform three steps up leads to family bedrooms above and to guest rooms. A tall, narrow bookcase is built into the wall of this staircase. There are a few practical books in both bookcases for Sybil; the rest are dummies. Matching brass plate light switches near each bookcase control all illumination; the chande-lier, the wall sconces above mantel and elsewhere, the desk lamp, etc. A door opening offstage Down extreme Right leads to patients' rooms in the asylum, to quarters for the attendants and the kitchen.

Ancient stone columns rise from behind the foot of each staircase and support the largest arch across the room's center. Concealed behind the Right col-umn and Right stairway wall is a low "jumping off", platform for one of Dracula's more informal arrivals. Upstage, beyond the main archway, the walls are panelled. One panel, in Right wall near upstage Right corner is a "secret panel" and swings open offstage for Dracula's blackout exit in Act Two. In Act Three this panel is used for the startling cape escape with stage lights full up. It is vital that this secret panel be low *so that Count Dracula must duck down to go through it, and that it be* not *much wider than he. With such dimensions the panel makes possible (along with cape action described later) his vanishing right before the eyes of the audience.*

Right Center below fireplace there is a comfortable sofa of the period, faced downstage on a slight angle. Left of the sofa is an end table with ashtray, etc. Left Center, below the bar, is a mahogany desk with a high backed desk chair behind it. It is this chair which moves on its own when the "invisible" Dracula sits at the desk in Act Three. And the center seat cushion of sofa is rigged to depress when the unseen Dracula "sits" on it and to spring back to full plumpness when he "rises."

Between sofa and desk there is a graceful swivel chair, non-office type, lightweight enough for easy shifting. A black 1930's French cradle telephone without dial on desk's Left end; a low decorative desk lamp on its Right end; a silver cigarette box with silver lighter nearby; a small electric push button buzzer on upstage Right end of desk. Below the Left stairway is an old-fashioned hassock or tuffet. A further archaic touch is the bell cord hanging on the wall Right of mantel.

AT RISE: *Ghostly ORGAN MUSIC starts as the HOUSE LIGHTS DIM OUT. CURTAIN RISES in BLACKOUT. From the dark there comes an ear shattering SCREAM. Fast ORGAN*

*GLISSANDO through top treble, then MUSIC
OUT. A second SCREAM and STAGE LIGHTS
COME UP FULL AND FAST.* SYBIL SEWARD
*is alone onstage out on the balcony, clutching the
railing with both hands.* HENNESSEY, *a middling-
young asylum attendant, runs on from Down Right.
He is earnest, trim, hard working and pleasant.*

HENNESSEY. Miss Seward! What is it?
SYBIL. (*Enters from balcony gasping.*) Oh, Hennes-
sey! I was leaning over the railing, watching for Mr.
Harker's motorcar—and I almost fell. Such a fright!
But don't tell Dr. Seward. (*Then, as a footnote.*) He's
my brother.
HENNESSEY. (*Politely patient.*) Miss Seward, I
know he's your brother.
SYBIL. Yes, I know you know, but I have to remind
myself. I forget things. Things and people and places.
Oh, well—! (*Shrugs, goes back to railing and leans
over at a dangerous angle.*)

(SYBIL SEWARD *is somewhere in her late forties, but
won't say where. She's a spinster, not neurotic,
just addle-pated. She is vague, occasionally detached from reality and harmlessly touched in the
head. Her hair is fussy, too girlish for her figure
and done in one of the more unfortunate styles
of the 1930's. Her bifocal glasses bounce on her
bosom, suspended by an ornate chain round her
neck. She wears her personal misconception of an
evening gown.*)

HENNESSEY. (*Hurries to her.*) Please be careful.
You'll lose your balance.
SYBIL. Oh, I lost that years ago. I was unbalanced
as a child. . . . Not a sign of Mr. Harker's motor. It's
possible he's been killed in an accident. Tsk, tsk! Who
will tell poor Mina?

HENNESSEY. Come inside, Miss. You could fall straight down to that concrete driveway. (*Tugging her arm.*) Miss Seward, please! It's a two hundred foot drop.

SYBIL. (*Puts on bifocals, glances over rail.*) I would be rather messy, wouldn't I? . . . Well, just look at that!

HENNESSEY. What?

SYBIL. There, across the valley. Castle Carfax with only one light burning. So strange. Night after night, in the top tower, it's the only sign of life. (*As he leads her into room.*) Hennessey, if you were as rich as Count Dracula, wouldn't you burn more than one light?

HENNESSEY. (*Guiding her toward sofa.*) Well, Miss, he's in only one room at a time.

SYBIL. It's puzzling. He dresses too well to be a pinchpenny.

HENNESSEY. Now don't fret, Miss. Sit down and I'll get you a nice sherry. (*He seats her on sofa, goes to bar.*)

SYBIL. Good! Just the thing for my twitchy nerves. (*Removes bifocals, swings them so they hang down her back.*) I'll need more than a dollop of sherry to put Count Dracula out of mind. He worries me.

HENNESSEY. (*Opens decanter, pours.*) He worries many people, Miss. I grant you, foreigners have foreign ways, but people in the village are afraid of him.

SYBIL. Afraid? Why?

HENNESSEY. They think he's—different. Odd, you know.

SYBIL. (*Taking sherry from him.*) No, I don't. I find him charming. Beautifully polite. The villagers would do well to copy his manners.

HENNESSEY. (*Closes door Down Right.*) Perhaps, Miss, but they think it strange that he's never seen in the daytime. Only at night. (*He tidies desk, straightens books in Left bookcase as they talk.*)

SYBIL. He's not odd, he's just new hereabouts. (*Sip-

ping sherry.) What matter whether he's seen at high noon or by moonlight? What distresses me is his living quite alone in that crumbling castle. I don't think he has servants.

HENNESSEY. None, Miss. The villagers won't work there. They say it's haunted.

SYBIL. How thrilling! (*A girlish laugh and she drains her glass, holds it out.*) Another sherry, please.

SEWARD. (*As he enters Down Left stairway.*) Not if you've had one already, Sybil.

SYBIL. (*Instant deflation.*) Oh, Arthur! You're such a spoil-sport. (*Thrusts glass at* HENNESSEY, *turns away pettishly.*)

SEWARD. Moderation, dear. Moderation's the thing. Besides, Hennessey has work to do and you have guests for dinner. (*He goes to her, adjusts her glasses so they hang over her bosom again.* DR. SEWARD *is a dignified, kindly, compassionate man in his mid-fifties. He wears black tie and dinner clothes.*) As I left the laboratory just now, Hennessey, I stopped by the dining room for a look at the table. Most attractive. My compliments.

HENNESSEY. Thank you, Dr. Seward.

SEWARD. (*To* SYBIL.) How is Mina?

SYBIL. (*Still annoyed.*) I haven't the slightest. I haven't seen her since lunch.

HENNESSEY. Miss Mina is a bit better, sir. Had good appetite when I took up her tea.

SEWARD. Oh? That's encouraging.

HENNESSEY. Let me fix you a highball, Doctor.

SEWARD. A small one. I'm on my way upstairs to see her now. (*While* HENNESSEY *blends whiskey and Seltzer water.*) Sybil, I wish you'd take more interest in Mina, especially now that she's so ill. She's your ward as well as mine.

SYBIL. I don't feel that, Brother. Whose signature is on the guardianship papers? Yours or mine?

SEWARD. Mine, but—

SYBIL. There, you see? I'm not important.

SEWARD. You loved her when she was a child, but now that she's grown—

SYBIL. I still love her—certain days of the week.

SEWARD. What do you mean, certain days?

SYBIL. Well, one week it's Monday-Wednesday-Friday; the next it could be Tuesday-Thursday-Saturday. I switch around. (*She rises, drifts to the window, looks out.*)

(*Both men look at her, then at each other in mild despair.* HENNESSEY *brings highball to* DR. SEWARD.)

SEWARD. Thank you. What do you suppose is keeping Mr. Harker?

SYBIL. He's dead on the highway.

SEWARD. (*Wheels to her in shock.*) *What?*

HENNESSEY. (*Softly.*) It's one of her pronouncements, sir.

SEWARD. Oh. (*Laughs.*) What a relief!

SYBIL. (*Comes down to him.*) Laugh if you like, but I have second sight.

SEWARD. Of course you have, dear, but sometimes it gets blurred through your bifocals. . . . Is Mr. Harker's room ready?

HENNESSEY. It is, sir, and Professor Van Helsing's. Let me check with you, Doctor. If Miss Mina feels strong enough to come downstairs for dinner, that will make it five at table?

SEWARD. I haven't counted noses. Let's see— (*Points to* SYBIL, *then to himself.*) One—two—and Mina and Harker and Van Helsing. Five. (HENNESSEY *nods, starts out Down Right.*)

SYBIL. Six.

SEWARD. How six?

SYBIL. (*Sits on sofa arm, swinging an abandoned leg.*) I invited Count Dracula.

SEWARD. Oh, *no!*

SYBIL. Oh, yes. He's the only Count in twenty miles and his visits lend us tone.

SEWARD. Well, too late to stop him. Six, Hennessey.

HENNESSEY. Yes, Doctor. I'll go set an extra place. (*Starts out Left this time and exits Up Left stairs.*)

(SEWARD *studies his sister a moment, sighs, goes to desk for cigarette.*)

SYBIL. (*Rising.*) Heigho! I think I'll have another sherry.

SEWARD. (*With a staying hand as she approaches bar.*) I think not. (SYBIL *pouts, flounces to sofa again and sits far Right end, her back to him.* SEWARD *lights cigarette, crosses to her.*) Sybil, I wish you hadn't invited Count Dracula. I don't like him—and he has an odd effect on Mina.

SYBIL. Of course he has. In his presence any red-blooded woman perks up. Why, even at my age, I— (*Touches her hair, then stops.*) He's mysterious and handsome and utterly Continental.

SEWARD. That's the facade. It's the man behind it I mistrust. There's something unwholesome about him which I can't quite— Have you ever shaken hands with him?

SYBIL. No, he always kisses my hand. No other man ever did. It makes me tingle.

SEWARD. Don't be absurd.

SYBIL. (*Hurt.*) There's nothing absurd about tingling. It's very pleasant.

SEWARD. I shook hands with him only once, the first time you brought him here. When was that?

SYBIL. Oh, a month ago. Shortly after he'd arrived in England.

SEWARD. I'll never forget that handshake. It was like ice. It was not the hand of a living man—more like the hand of the dead.

SYBIL. (*Rises after a horrified stare.*) Arthur, how dreadful! You're trying to make me dislike him.

SEWARD. Now, Sybil, dear—

SYBIL. Sh-hh! Wait. I heard a motorcar.

SEWARD. I didn't.

SYBIL. I have very sharp ears. (*She hurries to balcony.*)

SEWARD. (*To himself.*) And second sight—and a mind like a steel trap.

SYBIL. (*Looks down over balcony railing.*) Yes, it's Mr. Harker getting out of his car. I can't wait to meet him. My, isn't he handsome!

SEWARD. How can you tell? All you can see is the crown of his head.

SYBIL. Well— (*Another lean, another look.*) —he has a full head of hair, so he must be handsome. I'll take the elevator down and let him in. (*She starts for Left stairs.*)

SEWARD. And I'll tell Mina he's here. A fiance is exactly the medicine she needs.

SYBIL. Arthur, wouldn't it be wonderful if Mr. Harker and I got stuck in the elevator?

SEWARD. Sybil! What a thing to say.

SYBIL. What I mean is—it would be such an easy way for two strangers to break the ice. (*Innocently.*) Who knows? Trapped in the elevator, we could become intimate friends in five minutes.

SEWARD. (*Without rancor.*) Oh, Sybil, you're disgusting.

SYBIL. (*A quiet revelation.*) No, I'm not. I'm just lonely. (*She exits up Left stairs. SEWARD watches her go, then mounts Right stairs.*)

(*Before he is out of sight, door Down Right opens and RENFIELD starts in, sees Seward on stairs and quickly retreats into Right hall, flattening himself against the open door. RENFIELD is a schizophrenic inmate of indeterminate age, small stature and cadaverous complexion. SEWARD stops on stairs, glances back toward Right door, then shrugs and exits above.* RENFIELD *slyly peeks around door frame, sees he is safe and laughs softly. Then, gibbering to himself, he slithers across the room, starts up Left stairs—but* VOICES *off Left make him freeze:)*

HENNESSEY. (*Off Left.*) Don't worry, Miss Seward. I'll be right here for the luggage when you bring Mr. Harker up. (*Then, as if to a small child:*) T-h-e-r-e you are. Now, push the Ground Floor button.

SYBIL. (*Off Left.*) Thank you. Last time I went right up to the roof. (*Suddenly a loud, clangorous institutional ALARM BELL sounds, continuing intermittently until cut-off cue.*)

HENNESSEY. (*Off.*) Watch it, Miss. Patient's escaped!

(*At the sound of the alarm bell,* RENFIELD *spins in terror, runs to French windows, darts through them, pulls them shut behind him, drops to his knees and crawls out of sight Left of windows.* HENNESSEY *enters Left, hastens down steps as* DR. SEWARD *appears on Right stair platform.*)

SEWARD. (*Loudly, above the bell.*) Another patient loose?

HENNESSEY. (*Shouting.*) Sounds like it, Doctor.

SEWARD. (*Calls toward off Right.*) Wesley! *Wesley!* Cut off that alarm! (*They both wait. The ALARM BELL STOPS. Then* SEWARD *starts down into the room.*) That's better. No sense in stirring up all the patients. Who is it this time?

HENNESSEY. I don't know, sir. I'll find out. (*Starts Down Right.*) Renfield, I'll wager.

SEWARD. Again? He escaped twice yesterday.

HENNESSEY. Twice is a low score for Renfield, sir. (*Stops en route.*) Last Thursday he made it four times. He's like a weasel. Sometimes it takes three of us to—

That's funny. Those windows were wide open a minute
ago. Doctor, did you—?

SEWARD. I've not been near them. Do you suppose
Renfield—?

HENNESSEY. (*Alarmed.*) Just what I'm thinking.

SEWARD. Oh, my God! If he's climbed over that railing— Quick! (*They run to windows.* HENNESSEY *gets
there first, flings them open, hurries to railing and peers
down. As he does,* RENFIELD *leaps from behind Left of
windows, whirls* HENNESSEY *around and throttles him,
bending him backward over railing.*) Renfield, stop!
Stop that, for the love of God! (SEWARD *grabs* REN-
FIELD *and hurls him into the room where he cowers.*
SEWARD *stands over him as* HENNESSEY, *choking and
gasping, stumbles into the room.*) Do you want the
strait jacket, Renfield? Shall I put you in solitary confinement?

RENFIELD. Oh, no, not that! Please, Doctor, not solitary!

SEWARD. Then get hold of yourself. Think! Hennessey is your friend, your keeper. He is good to you.

RENFIELD. (*Begins to sob, clutching* SEWARD *round
the legs.*) No one is good to me. No one! I have no
friends. No family—no hope—no future.

SEWARD. Now, now, none of that. Self pity only
weakens a man. You've got to be strong.

HENNESSEY. (*Painfully massaging his neck.*) Oh,
Doctor, not any stronger.

SEWARD. Hennessey, ring that buzzer on the desk.
Get Wesley in here. One long buzz and three shorts—
or is it the reverse? (HENNESSEY, *after another choking spasm, mutely holds up three fingers, then one,
leans on desk and pushes buzzer.*) You've been improv-
ing a lot recently, Renfield. (*Lifts him to his feet.*) If
you behave yourself and respond to treatment, who
knows? In a year or two perhaps you can go home.

RENFIELD. (*Stops crying, wipes his eyes with his*

sleeve.) Home? I never had one. (*Turns abruptly, walks away to the fireplace.*)

SEWARD. But if you slip back into violence, as you did just now, it means—

RENFIELD. (*Sits hunched up on high stool by the fireplace.*) I know, Doctor. It means I descend further and further into madness. I don't know what happened. It was as though some evil voice told me to— Forgive me, Mr. Hennessey. I'm sorry, Doctor. I'll be good. Really I will. (*Begins bouncing on stool, sing-songs like a child:*) I'll be good, I'll be good. I'll be good, *good, GOOD!* (*Then hides his face in mantel corner.*)

(WESLEY, *a young attendant, makes a running entrance from Down Right.*)

WESLEY. You buzzed for me, Doctor?

SEWARD. Wesley, help Hennessey with Renfield. Get him back to his room. Now go along, Renfield. If you cooperate, we'll give you a reward. (*The two men ease a now placid* RENFIELD *from the stool and start Right with him.*) He's all right now.

HENNESSEY. Yes, sir, all right till next time.

RENFIELD. (*Stops, both feet planted.*) No, wait. Please wait. Dr. Seward, may I have my reward now?

SEWARD. Well—what would you like?

RENFIELD. Sugar. I'd like some sugar for my window sill.

SEWARD. Why?

RENFIELD. If I have to explain it, I don't want it.

HENNESSEY. He uses it to attract flies, sir.

SEWARD. Flies?

HENNESSEY. Tell him, Wesley.

WESLEY. Well, Dr. Seward, he catches flies and he eats them.

SEWARD. Good God!

WESLEY. Oh, he doesn't eat them all. Some he feeds to his spiders to fatten them up, and then—

SEWARD. (*Waits.*) And then?

WESLEY. Tell him, Hennessey.

HENNESSEY. He eats the spiders, sir.

RENFIELD. (*Begins to laugh.*) Yes, yes! I eat them. They are bits of life. They make me strong. Their little drops of blood give me *power.* (*Shouting.*) *Power over my enemies!* (*Instantly he tries to fight free of* HENNESSEY *and* WESLEY. *They tighten their holds and drag him off Down Right, thrashing, kicking, screaming.*)

SEWARD. (*Sits on desk edge, head in his hands.*) Poor devil. How can I help him?

SYBIL. (*Trills from off Left.*) This way, Mr. Harker, and we'll have a drink to toast our meeting! (*She enters Left, sees* SEWARD *and stops dead on the stairs. Her ingenue voice drops an octave.*) Oh, *Arthur!* I thought you were upstairs. (*Recovers, starts down steps.*) Mr. Harker is here and he's a perfect lamb!

(*As* DR. SEWARD *rises, comes forward and dons the host's welcoming smile—*JONATHAN HARKER *enters Left with briefcase and a commodious overnight case. He wears an impeccable business suit, is young, likable, muscular and glows with good health.*)

JONATHAN. Well, not quite a lamb, Miss Seward. More likely the family black sheep. (*Descending, puts luggage down, goes to* SEWARD *with hand outstretched.*) Good evening, Dr. Seward. Glad to see you again, sir.

SEWARD. (*Through handshake.*) Not one tenth as glad as I am to see you. I count on you to be the elixir to make Mina well.

JONATHAN. How is she?

SEWARD. (*Hedging.*) Oh, better. A bit better today.

SYBIL. I disagree. She looks worse. If you ask me, she's sinking fast.

JONATHAN. *Doctor!*

SEWARD. Pay no attention. Here, why don't you—

JONATHAN. (*Cuts in.*) I'd like to see her, please. Your telephone call of last night has worried me ever since, and now, what your sister says makes it sound— May I go up to her?

SEWARD. In a moment. I must talk to you first. (*Leads him up to bar.*) Here, mix yourself a drink. You need it after that long drive from London. . . . Sybil, shouldn't you make a last minute check in the dining room? (*Nods meaningfully to Left.*)

SYBIL. (*Settling on sofa.*) There's nothing to check. Hennessey did everything. All I was allowed to do was roll the napkins.

(JONATHAN *obediently mixes himself a drink he does not want, his attention divided between his host and his unusual hostess.*)

SEWARD. (*In full control, but in italics.*) Well, please go *somewhere* and do *something!* I want to speak to Jonathan privately. Go give us some music on the organ.

SYBIL. I can't. The keys are sticky.

SEWARD. How do you mean—sticky?

SYBIL. Well, yesterday I was playing a bit of Bach with my right hand— (*She waits.* JONATHAN *pauses in his mixing.*)

SEWARD. Yes?

SYBIL. And eating a jelly sandwich with my left— (*She shrugs.*)

SEWARD. I see. I'll get Wesley to clean the keyboard.

SYBIL. The jelly is mostly in the bass. (*Studies her hands a moment, then looks up brightly.*) Perhaps, if I put on gloves— (JONATHAN *lowers his drink in astonishment.*)

SEWARD. (*Takes* SYBIL'S *arm, gets her to her feet.*) Sybil, please. Go upstairs. Tell Mina Jonathan is waiting and help her dress for dinner. (*He propels her toward Right stairs.*)

SYBIL. (*Affronted.*) It appears we must all be your

minions! *Do* excuse me, Mr. Harker. (*She sweeps grandly up the steps and exits.*)

SEWARD. (*After a moment.*) I don't know whether Mina ever told you about my sister or not.

JONATHAN. A little. She said there were times when Miss Seward was—not quite herself.

SEWARD. Not-quite-herself. How kindly you put it. (*Turns, looks up Right stairway.*)

JONATHAN. (*A short embarrassed pause.*) Let me fix you a drink, Doctor.

SEWARD. No. We must talk of Mina—but have your own, of course.

JONATHAN. I don't really want it, sir. Please! Is she better or—? (SEWARD *indicates that* JONATHAN *sit on sofa, then pulls small swivel chair over and sits nearby.*)

SEWARD. Mina's spells of unaccountable weakness began one evening about a month ago. We'd had a guest for dinner—— By God, the same unwelcome man who's dining here tonight! (*Glances over his shoulder toward castle.*)

JONATHAN. Who?

SEWARD. Oh, a foreign Count poor Sybil thinks she's enamored of. Bogus, I'm sure. . . . Anyway, after dinner, he asked Mina to show him our rose garden. When they returned she was obviously ill. Her eyes were glazed. She faltered when she walked, she complained that her throat hurt badly and she felt very weak. Sybil put her to bed while I got rid of the Count—— No, wait. I don't remember his actual departure. (*Rises, goes to windows, looks off for a moment at the castle.*) How absurd. I was distracted by Mina's condition, of course, but come to think of it, it's as though he just melted from sight. . . . Well, that's nonsense. (*Comes down to desk.*) Would you like a cigarette?

JONATHAN. (*Shaking his head.*) Was she all right the next morning?

SEWARD. (*Getting cigarette for himself.*) No. It took two days for her to recover. She was fine for several days, then it happened again. Each time this strange lethargy would overcome her. It was hard to rouse her from sleep, to get her to eat, to hold her attention. The symptoms are those of anemia, but her illness is not anemia. It's baffling—and beyond my medical knowledge.

JONATHAN. How many attacks has she—?

SEWARD. Six, in four weeks. (*Sits, unlighted cigarette idle in his hand.*) I've had specialists up from London, she's had every test known to modern science, all without satisfaction. We have a hundred questions; no solutions.

JONATHAN. (*With no attempt at humor.*) I've changed my mind about that drink. (*Rises, gets his glass from bar.*) Six attacks? How many times has this Count—er—?

SEWARD. Dracula. Count Dracula. That's his castle across the valley. (*As* JONATHAN *goes to windows to look, the castle TOWER LIGHT FLICKERS RAPIDLY.*)

JONATHAN. Where the tower light is flickering? (*TOWER LIGHT GOES OUT.*) I mean—where it just went out?

SEWARD. (*Turns in swivel chair.*) It's out? God, that means he's on his way. (*Lights cigarette.*) He's an expatriate of Transylvania, wherever that may be.

JONATHAN. The Carpathian Mountains, I believe. (*Comes down with his drink.*) Has he seen Mina often? Perhaps visited here before these attacks?

SEWARD. Oh, he's turned up unexpectedly two or three evenings. I don't remember. Why?

JONATHAN. I'm clutching straws, of course, but— (*Sits, leans toward* SEWARD.) could there be any connection?

SEWARD. Between the Count and her illness? How could there be? If she were a romantic young thing, pining away with a school-girl crush, yes, possibly. I wish it were that simple. . . . Jonathan, I know you love her, your engagement has been announced, you plan to marry—

JONATHAN. In six weeks.

SEWARD. All of which makes it most difficult to tell you—

JONATHAN. (*A pause. Slowly puts his drink down on end table.*) To tell me—?

SEWARD. These spells, each progressively worse, could prove fatal.

JONATHAN. Mina! (*He goes quickly to Right stairs, looks up, turns to* SEWARD.) Then she is in great danger.

SEWARD. (*Nods assent.*) I've hesitated to tell you the most frightening aspect, but you must be told. A young friend of Mina's, Lucy Westenra, a girl just Mina's age and with exactly the same symptoms, died last week.

JONATHAN. (*Slowly approaches* SEWARD.) Where?

SEWARD. In this county, two miles away. We don't know yet, but it's possible—just possible, mind you— that Lucy Westenra's case and Mina's could be the beginning of an epidemic.

JONATHAN. (*Grips him by the arms.*) Dr. Seward, my God, my God! What can we do?

SEWARD. (*Disengages* JONATHAN'S *hands, puts an arm about his shoulder.*) First, we can't afford panic. (*As* JONATHAN *starts away,* SEWARD *detains him.*) Listen to me! Lucy was frail and tubercular all her life. She lacked the stamina to fight back. But Mina has had blooming health since babyhood. She—

JONATHAN. (*Suddenly breaks, his face averted.*) Doctor, if we lose her I shall die.

SEWARD. (*Leads him to sofa, sits by him.*) Now, now, we won't lose her. The man who can save her arrives here tonight. He's my old friend, Professor Heinrich Van Helsing.

JONATHAN. (*Turns so* SEWARD *won't see him dry his eyes with his fists.*) Van Helsing? The Dutch specialist?

SEWARD. The same. We graduated from medical college together. Today he's one of the world's foremost authorities on rare diseases. I sent him Mina's full medical report and Lucy Westenra's case history. Last night he phoned from Amsterdam that he was on his way. He's known Mina since she was a child and—

JONATHAN. (*One hand up to interrupt him.*) Can he save her?

SEWARD. (*A barely perceptible hesitation.*) I stake my life on it.

SYBIL. (*Off Right upstairs.*) Careful, dear. You haven't been downstairs in three days. Slowly now, Mina. Slow-*ly!* (JONATHAN *rises, goes to staircase.* SEWARD *returns swivel chair to original position.*)

(MINA *appears descending the Right stairs, her progress hindered by* SYBIL'S *death grip. Despite illness and pallor,* MINA MURRAY *is a most attractive young woman, becomingly gowned in a long flowing chiffon, low cut evening dress of striking hue. Her abundant hair is piled high, her earrings are both simple and elegant. At her neck she wears an old fashioned cameo on a wide velvet "choker" which matches her gown and conceals the lower part of her throat.*)

MINA. Jonathan, dear!

JONATHAN. Mina! You look beautiful, darling! Not sick at all.

MINA. I feel fine. Just a little weak.

JONATHAN. (*Takes her arm.*) Here, let me help you.

MINA. No, truly, I don't need help.

SYBIL. Yes, she does. If I let go, she'd slump right to the floor!

JONATHAN. I have her, Miss Seward. Sit here, darling. (*He guides* MINA *into Right corner of the sofa. As he goes above sofa to come around and sit by her,* SYBIL *crosses below sofa, plops herself down at* MINA'S *Left side, leaving* JONATHAN *neatly thwarted.*)

SEWARD. *(Tries to catch* SYBIL's *eye.)* Oh, Sybil?

SYBIL. *(Spreading her gown, taking up more room.)* Yes, Brother?

SEWARD. Nothing. *(*JONATHAN *gets tuffet from downstage Left, carries it to Right of sofa, sits on it near* MINA. SYBIL *watches affably, unaware that she is a cul-de-sac for Cupid.)*

SYBIL. Now, everybody comfy? . . . You're right, Mr. Harker. She does look well. *(Puts on her bifocals and studies* MINA.) Oh, I see. It's make-up.

SEWARD. Sybil, *come have a sherry!*

SYBIL. *(Instantly on her feet.)* Oh, jolly! I was just beginning to flag a bit. *(She goes to bar where* SEWARD *gives her a sherry and a glare.* JONATHAN *moves over, sits by* MINA, *patting her hand affectionately.* SYBIL *starts back toward sofa but is detoured by* SEWARD *into the swivel chair.)*

JONATHAN. I've been terribly worried about you.

MINA. No need, darling. Now that you're here, just watch me astound the medical profession. It will be known as The Mina Murray Cure, or Instant Recovery.

JONATHAN. *(Laughing, embraces her.)* Oh, dearest, dearest Mina!

SYBIL. *(Squinting at wristwatch.)* I wonder if Count Dracula has stepped into a quagmire?

SEWARD. Why on earth would he?

SYBIL. Well, he *could,* you know, if he walked through the woods. He's late.

MINA. *(Gets out of* JONATHAN's *embrace, sits forward, spine erect, staring oddly.)* But he *is* coming?

JONATHAN. Mina, what is it? You like this man?

MINA. *(A moment.)* No. He fascinates me, but I don't like him.

JONATHAN. *(After a puzzled glance at* SEWARD.) Oh, I almost forgot. I brought you a present. *(Goes to briefcase, takes out oblong plush jewelry box.)*

SYBIL. Oh, how nice! *(Under her breath to* SEWARD:) Is today Mina's birthday?

SEWARD. (*Patting her shoulder.*) No, dear.

JONATHAN. Here, darling.

MINA. A jewel case! Oh, Jonathan, you've done something you shouldn't.

JONATHAN. I don't know why not. It's just another way to say I love you. Go on, open it.

MINA. (*Lifts out a triple strand of pearls.*) Jonathan! They're *exquisite!* (*Murmurs of approval from* SYBIL *and* SEWARD. JONATHAN *steps behind sofa, reaches for clasp of* MINA'S *velvet choker.*)

JONATHAN. Dear, let me take this off. Let's see how they look on you.

(SOUND: *Fade in DOGS HOWLING in distance.*)

MINA. (*Covering throat with both hands.*) No! *Don't!*

JONATHAN. But, darling, why not?

MINA. I mean not now. Not—not in this dress. Pearls don't really go well with— *Tomorrow!* Tomorrow I'll—I'll wear a different gown for dinner and they'll— They're lovely, Jonathan, and I thank you— but don't ask me to put them on. Not yet. When I'm really well, I'll— (*She begins to cry.*)

(SOUND: *DOGS HOWLING grows LOUDER.* SEWARD *and* SYBIL *glance toward window but do not move.*)

JONATHAN. (*Sitting quickly, cradles her.*) Of course, Mina. Of course you don't have to wear them now. Here, darling. (*Gives her his breast pocket handkerchief.*)

MINA. I'm shivering. Hold me close, Jonathan. There's a cold wind blowing round me.

SYBIL. (*Rises, starts Left.*) Perhaps the hall window is open.

SEWARD. It isn't. Please get her a shawl. Sybil.

(SYBIL *turns, starts toward Right stairs. ALL LIGHTS FLICKER OFF and ON rapidly, then ON AGAIN. Involuntarily everyone looks up at chandelier.*)

(SOUND: *HOWLING INCREASES and seems NEARER, a great melancholy chorus, deep throated, sustained and terrifying.*)

MINA. Listen!

SYBIL. (*Stopped on first step.*) It's as though every dog for miles around is—is trying to warn us. Arthur, you remember mother's superstition about dogs howling in the night? She said it meant someone nearby—would die before morning.

MINA. (*Pushing free of JONATHAN, leans forward, staring again.*) No, they're wolves. They sound like wolves! (MINA *rises as though mesmerized, moves slowly to the windows and stands motionless, looking out.*)

JONATHAN. (*Following her.*) There are no wolves here, Mina darling.

MINA. How still it is down there. Not a leaf stirring. Sybil is right. It's like death.

(SOUND: *The HOWLING begins to FADE AWAY, overlapped and replaced by EERIE MUSIC of The Dracula Leitmotif. ALL LIGHTS FLICKER AGAIN and GO OUT, leaving only the glow from the fireplace and a dim light from Left hallway, spilling down the stairs.*)

SYBIL. (*Frightened, goes to SEWARD.*) Arthur! What is it?

SEWARD. (*Crossing below her to Right.*) The electric power. Don't be alarmed. I'll try the switch. (*He flicks wall switch by Right bookcase several times.*) Nothing. It must be the main fuse.

(*MUSIC SWELLS as* COUNT DRACULA *enters at top of Left stairway, his shadow rippling down the steps. His countenance is arresting, lupine, cruel and coldly handsome. He is immaculately attired in white tie and tails. Over his shoulders is an evening cape of costly black satin lined with vibrant red silk and with a stiff, high standing collar which frames his head.* DRACULA *holds his silk opera hat inverted in one hand and drops his white kid gloves into it with a gesture that is the quintessence of arrogance. When he speaks his accent is slightly Continental and his voice not only insinuates but threatens.*)

DRACULA. (*A mocking bow.*) Good evening. (*MU-SIC DIES OUT. They all turn to him in surprise and* MINA *comes away from the windows, looking at him fixedly.*)

SEWARD. (*Holds near Right bookcase.*) Good evening. (*As* DRACULA *comes down the steps,* SYBIL *crosses to him.*)

SYBIL. Count Dracula, how good of you to come. We're sorry about the lights.

DRACULA. The lights?

SYBIL. They seem to have quite gone out. Quite.

DRACULA. (*Kissing her hand.*) What matter? You illuminate the room. (*He looks at the chandelier, makes the most casual of gestures toward it and instantly ALL STAGE LIGHTS COME UP FULL.*)

SYBIL. Oh, good! *There* they are. Now why do you suppose they went off?

DRACULA. (*Shrugs.*) Perhaps a case of temporary electrical indisposition. (*Puts silk hat with gloves on desk, crosses to* MINA, *bends over her hand and kisses it.*) My dear Miss Murray, how beautiful you are to-night. You are a feast—for the eyes.

MINA. We—we are honored to have you with us.

DRACULA. It is I who am honored, to be your guest and that of the eminent Doctor and his interesting sister. And this gentleman—?

MINA. Is my fiance. Count Dracula, may I present Mr. Jonathan Harker?

JONATHAN. (*Holds out his hand.*) How do you do?

DRACULA. (*Ignores the proffered hand.*) Ah, yes. The young architect.

JONATHAN. (*Mild surprise.*) How did you know? Did Mina—?

MINA. No. I never mentioned it. (*All four look at him curiously.*)

DRACULA. I surmised. You look like an architect, Mr. Harker. You yourself are so symmetrically built.

SEWARD. Sybil, take Count Dracula's cape and hat, please. Hang them in the hall while I fix him a drink. (SYBIL *starts immediately for* DRACULA, *arms raised to remove his cape.*)

DRACULA. If you will permit me, Doctor— (*Gracefully steps aside, dodging the oncoming* SYBIL.) *and* Miss Seward, I'll retain the cape. There's a chill in the autumn air. As for the libation, thank you, no. I never drink—socially. (SYBIL *gets his hat and gloves from the desk.* DRACULA *gives her a lordly wave of dismissal. She all but curtseys, floats up the Left stairs, hat clutched to her bosom, and exits.* DRACULA *moves to French windows, stands in profile looking out.* JONATHAN *goes to* MINA, *reaching for her hand but she draws away.*)

MINA. Don't, Jonathan. Not now. (*She crosses to fireplace, watching* DRACULA, *leaving* JONATHAN *puzzled and hurt.*)

DRACULA. What an interesting vista. From here my castle looks like a huge, crumbling tombstone.

SYBIL. (*Enters Left stairs, descends breathlessly.*) Arthur, there's a car coming up the drive. I spotted it through the hall window.

SEWARD. (*Starts for French windows.*) Good. It's bound to be my old friend from Holland.

SYBIL. Professor—

SYBIL AND DRACULA. (*Together.*) Heinrich Van

Helsing. (*Though they started in spoken duet,* DRACULA *finishes the name alone,* SYBIL'S *voice having faded away in her astonishment.*)

SEWARD. Why—yes.

DRACULA. (*As though searching memory.*) In a rather ancient motorcar which he keeps in London— for his frequent trips from Amsterdam—to confer with your English specialists.

SEWARD. Why, how— Are you clairvoyant? (DRACULA *smiles, shakes his head.*) How do you know these things?

DRACULA. Merely a hobby. I collect facts, trivial or momentous, and store them away for future use.

SEWARD. I see. Excuse me. I'll go let him in. (SEWARD *crosses to Left stairs, stops part way up for another look at his baffling guest, then exits above.* DRACULA *steps out onto balcony, holding out the edges of his cape at the railing, making him resemble a great black bat blotting out the sky. Trance-like,* MINA *moves closer to the windows watching him.*)

SYBIL. Mr. Harker, I'll ring for an attendant to take your luggage upstairs. (*She starts toward bell cord.*) You must want to change for dinner.

JONATHAN. (*Half hears, studying* MINA.) To change?—Oh, yes, of course. Don't bother to ring, Miss Seward. (*Getting his luggage.*) I'll take my things up myself. Which room is it?

SYBIL. It's at the end of the passage. It— I'd better show you. You might get it mixed up with the linen closet. (*She notices jewelry case and pearls on sofa, scoops them up.*) You may as well take these along. I don't believe Mina likes your gift. Pity. (*She sails ahead of him, starts up Right stairway.*)

JONATHAN. (*Another glance at* MINA *whose back is to him.*) Perhaps not. She's behaving very strangely.

SYBIL. Oh, this is one of her *good* days. Come along, Mr. Harker. (SYBIL *beckons with the jewel case, exits above and* JONATHAN *follows her with luggage. In-*

stantly DRACULA *whirls and faces* MINA. *His movement is so sudden she draws back with a gasp.*)

DRACULA. Ah, Miss Murray, we are alone. How op-
portune. (*Takes her hand, leads her toward sofa.*) You
seem perturbed, my dear. I want you to sit down, empty
your mind of all trepidation.

MINA. (*Slowly pulls her hand free, starts toward
desk chair.*) I'll—I'll sit here, Count Dracula.

DRACULA. (*Takes her by both hands, gently but in-
exorably leads her to sofa, seats her.*) Please. I know
what is best for a lovely convalescent. T-r-u-s-t me, my
dear. Relax. Lean back and close your eyes. (*His voice,
his hypnotic eyes have a mesmeric effect on* MINA. *She
does exactly as told.* DRACULA *gives the chandelier a
glance and a casual gesture and ALL LIGHTS GO
OUT except fire glow, faint off stage hall lights and
the feeble light of distant stars. OMINOUS MUSIC
begins softly. He looks down triumphantly upon the unseeing* MINA, *glides to above sofa and stands directly
behind her.*) There, that's better, isn't it? The gloom is
soothing to your beautiful, tired eyes. (*Adjusts her
head, unfastens her neck band and cameo.*) Let me remove this velvet choker. It is constrictive and conceals
your lovely throat.

MINA. (*Weakly, her protesting hands go to her
throat.*) No, no—

DRACULA. Sh-hh! You must be absolutely still. You
must rest. R-e-l-a-x. (*He drops choker on floor behind
sofa, murmuring hypnotically:*) You are going to sleep
—to sleep—a quiet, dreamless sleep. You are floating,
drifting through space—now you are falling, slowly,
slowly—falling into oblivion! (MINA *gives a little sigh
and her head rolls to one side. She is asleep. MUSIC
SURGES slightly and* DRACULA *begins to laugh. Then
he bares his teeth in a hideous grin, slowly lowers his
head toward* MINA'S *throat, his jaws working like an
animal salivating over raw meat. Just as he is above her
throat,* HENNESSEY *enters Left stairs with a small re-*

freshment tray, snaps on wall switch by Left bookcase on his way down steps. STAGE LIGHTS UP FULL. MUSIC OUT. With a snarl of fury, DRACULA leaps back.)

HENNESSEY. (*Offering tray.*) Canapes, sir?

DRACULA. (*A thunderclap of contempt.*) Canapes! (*He wheels, strides out onto balcony, stands breathing heavily, livid at the interruption. HENNESSEY starts toward MINA with tray, sees she is asleep, puts tray on desk. He moves tuffet from Right of sofa to downstage of desk and goes up Left steps quietly and exits. MINA stirs, sits up with effort, palms pressed to her brow.*)

MINA. What a horrible dream!

DRACULA. (*Turns.*) A dream?

MINA. A nightmare. I dreamed that I was powerless, unable to defend myself—as a giant bat was about to attack my throat—and draw my blood.

DRACULA. How interesting. You've had this dream before?

MINA. Yes, several times. That's what frightens me. I feel as though it is not a dream—but real.

DRACULA. The subconscious mind is often overactive. (*MINA's hands go to her throat. She discovers the velvet choker is missing, looks for it on the sofa, then rises frantically.*)

MINA. My cameo and velvet band! They're gone.

DRACULA. An heirloom, no doubt? What a pity. (*As MINA searches downstage of sofa, DRACULA smiles evilly and walks out of sight Left on balcony. MINA, without seeing him depart, looks above sofa, finds choker on floor. With trembling fingers she is trying to fasten it around her neck as DR. SEWARD enters on Left stair platform carrying an old battered suitcase and a venerable Gladstone bag. He is followed by PROFESSOR HEINRICH VAN HELSING whose attire is as outdated as his luggage.*)

SEWARD. Mina! Look who's here!

VAN HELSING. Ah-h-h, dear little Wilhelmina! How

long has it been? (MINA, *nervously holding choker with left hand to conceal her throat, extends her right hand as* VAN HELSING *approaches. He surprises her with an embrace instead of a handshake and she drops choker.* VAN HELSING *releases her, then holds her at arms' length.*) You've grown into a beauty, as I predicted. Remember, Arthur? When she was a knee-high ugly duckling I prophesied a swan. (*He stands back to look at her.* MINA *stoops to pick up choker but he cups her chin, lifts her to full height and studies her face:*) You're pale, of course, but one of those rare, lucky women on whom pallor is an adornment. It makes your skin translucent. (HEINRICH VAN HELSING *is a few years older than* DR. SEWARD, *a genial, warmhearted man except when crossed over an issue he deems important. Then geniality is replaced by sternness. His tie is askew, his suit, like his hair, is rumpled and it's a safe bet there's no tuxedo in his luggage.*)

MINA. (*Abstractedly.*) Dear Professor Van Helsing, it's good to see you again.

SEWARD. I'll send your luggage upstairs, Heinrich, and you can change for dinner.

VAN HELSING. Change? I brought no change. This is it! I put a napkin here— (*Tucks finger in collar.*) and I am ready. (SEWARD *smiles, puts luggage below desk.* MINA *starts to stoop for choker but* VAN HELSING *anticipates her and picks it up.*) Ah, this cameo is old. Was it your mother's?

MINA. (*Reaching for it.*) Yes. I inherited it when she—

VAN HELSING. Let me put it on for you. (MINA *turns for him to fasten it at the back of her neck, but he turns her round to face him again.*) No, face me. Face me. I want to see you when I talk. And take your hands away from your throat. They're in my way. . . . Ah, your pretty mother. You were too young to even remember her when she died, but I remem— (*Stops, looks closely at base of her throat, draws back with a hissing intake of breath. Instantly* MINA'S *hands cover her throat again.*)

SEWARD. What's wrong?

VAN HELSING. (*Moves her hands aside, looks more closely, separates her now clenched hands and drops choker into them.*) Sit down, Wilhelmina. We must talk.

MINA. No, Professor, *no!* Not now! Later—after dinner, or—

VAN HELSING. (*Quietly.*) *Now,* Wilhelmina. (*He sits on sofa, draws* MINA *down beside him.*)

SEWARD. What's the matter?

VAN HELSING. At the moment, merely a suspicion as to what ails your pretty ward, an explanation for this anemia that is not anemia. . . . Mina, my dear, since when have you had those two little wounds at the base of your throat?

MINA. A—a few days. Last week, perhaps. . . . I don't remember. (SEWARD *pulls swivel chair near sofa, sits looking from one to the other. Unnoticed by any of them,* DRACULA *appears at the open windows and listens intently, scowling.*)

VAN HELSING. And how did you get these two little wounds? (*Still unobserved,* DRACULA *steps into the room, his look concentrated on* MINA. *He pantomimes putting on a neck scarf, fastening it with a pin.* MINA, *who has been nervously twisting her hands, stops. Her face lights up with relief; she has received the thought transference.*)

MINA. It was an accident. I was fastening my scarf with a brooch which has a long, very sharp pin and—

VAN HELSING. I should like to see that brooch with that long, sharp pin. (DRACULA'S *face contorts with anger. He steps toward the Professor, his hands claw-like, reaching out, but he stops, again concentrating his attention on* MINA.)

MINA. (*As though just recalling.*) I'm afraid I've lost it.

VAN HELSING. I see.

SEWARD. Is it important?

VAN HELSING. The pin, no. The little wounds, yes. (DRACULA *now extends one hand toward* MINA, *then toward Right stairs and back to her. She rises slowly, her voice little more than a whisper:*)

MINA. Please, will you excuse me? I must go upstairs and rest a little before dinner. (*As she mounts Right stairway and exits, the two men follow to base of steps and watch her off.* DRACULA *moves as silently as a jungle cat and leans against column at base of Left stairs, arms folded, cape enshrouding all but his mocking face.* SEWARD *and* VAN HELSING, *still at Right stairs looking after* MINA, *do not yet see him.*)

VAN HELSING. She is lying. No brooch, no long sharp pin caused those wounds.

SEWARD. But, Heinrich, they are just tiny white dots.

VAN HELSING. With little red centers. You saw? Yes, but you don't know what caused them. None of your London specialists could tell you. But *I* will tell you— (*Stops as he sees* DRACULA.) We have an eavesdropper.

DRACULA. (*Smiles urbanely.*) Dr. Seward, won't you introduce us?

SEWARD. Oh, I'm sorry. I didn't hear you come in.

DRACULA. Evidently.

SEWARD. (*Bringing* VAN HELSING *toward him.*) Count Dracula, may I present my old friend, Professor Heinrich Van Helsing.

DRACULA. Good evening, Professor.

VAN HELSING. Good evening. (*Neither makes a move to shake hands.*) I know your name.

DRACULA. You flatter me.

VAN HELSING. Not really. There was an infamous Count Voivode Dracula who ruled Transylvania in the Fourteenth Century.

DRACULA. Possibly an ancestor. . . . Infamous, you say?

VAN HELSING. A descendant of Atilla the Hun. Some historians claim he was a Vampire.

DRACULA. (*A moment, then a polite smile.*) What an unusual occupation.

(SYBIL *starts down Right stairs carrying a small ostrich feather fan which clashes with her dress. She turns, calls back up:*)

SYBIL. Come along, Mr. Harker. We must let her rest.

JONATHAN. (*Off Right.*) Be right down, Miss Seward.

SYBIL. Dr. Van Helsing—I mean, Professor. How nice to see you. I can never remember whether to call you Doctor or Professor.

VAN HELSING. (*Patting her hand kindly.*) Try them alternately. I'm bound to respond to one or the other.

SYBIL. Count Dracula, I hope you won't mind if dinner's delayed? Mina has to rest a bit longer.

DRACULA. Don't be concerned. Food interests me not at all. Generally I— (*Searching for the word.*) sup much later.

VAN HELSING. I mind. I'm famished.

SYBIL. Come along, then, have some canapes. They're quite fattening. (*She leads him to hors d'oeuvre tray on desk. As he reaches for food, she whips feather fan open, rapidly swishes it above canapes.*) Oh, dear!

SEWARD. What is it?

SYBIL. A housefly! Why don't you scientists get rid of them? You've had *centuries* to make some effort.

VAN HELSING. We get sidetracked by larger forms of life. (*Waves fly aside, munches canapes.*)

JONATHAN. (*Enters down Right stairs in tuxedo.*) I looked in on Mina. I think she's asleep.

SEWARD. Good. Come meet Professor Van Helsing. Heinrich, this is Jonathan Harker, Mina's fiance.

JONATHAN. How do you do? (JONATHAN's *hand*

shoots out as usual but VAN HELSING, *with a canape in each of his own, can't grasp it. He crams both canapes into his mouth and shakes hands.*)

VAN HELSING. (*Muffled by crackers and cheese.*) Mina's-a-lucky-girl. Fine-specimen.

JONATHAN. (*Laughing.*) What did you say, sir?

VAN HELSING. (*Swallows, speaks clearly.*) I said Mina has good taste. You're a fine, healthy young animal.

JONATHAN. (*Embarrassed.*) Oh. Thank you. (*To* SYBIL.) I guess that ties in with your lamb theory.

SYBIL. (*Vaguely; she's forgotten it.*) What? Oh, yes.

DRACULA. Professor Van Helsing, just before we were introduced, you were about to give Dr. Seward your diagnosis of Miss Murray's ailment. May we hear it now?

VAN HELSING. No, you may not. I don't discuss such matters with laymen.

DRACULA. Layman? You call me that? (*Laughs.*) How very amusing. I have been called much worse. (*He goes to fireplace, coldly observing them all, his arms spread wide across the mantel and holding his cape, all but obliterating the fireplace itself.*)

VAN HELSING. I see I'm the only one not in formal dress. I'd better eat in the kitchen.

SEWARD. (*Smiles at him.*) No, we'll give you an oversized napkin, cover you head to foot.

JONATHAN. (*Opening cigarette case.*) Would anyone like a smoke?

SYBIL. Oh, I'd love it. I don't smoke well, but it makes me look so worldly. (*As* JONATHAN *lights it for her she coughs on the first puff.*)

JONATHAN. Anyone else? Professor?

VAN HELSING. No, I have my pipe— (*Feels in pockets without success.*) somewhere.

JONATHAN. (*Approaching him.*) Count Dracula?

DRACULA. (*Cuttingly.*) I have my own. (*They settle down.* VAN HELSING *gives up his pipe search, sits in*

swivel chair; SEWARD *sits at desk munching;* JONA-
THAN *and* SYBIL *are on sofa with their cigarettes. All
have their backs to* DRACULA *as, from thin air, he magically produces a cigarette with its tip literally flaming.*
VAN HELSING *arcs in swivel chair just in time to catch
this peripherally. As* DRACULA *blows flame out, puts
cigarette to his lips and begins smoking,* VAN HELSING
rises, crosses to him.)

VAN HELSING. What an unusual cigarette. It smells
of sulphur.

DRACULA. That must have been the match I used.

VAN HELSING. (*Evenly.*) I did not see you use a
match. (*There is an unblinking stare between them.
Then* DRACULA *goes swiftly to* SYBIL *and bows.*)

DRACULA. Miss Seward, you once said I must see the
view of Castle Carfax from your roof. I should like
you to show it to me. *Now.*

SYBIL. Why, I'd be delighted. We can have a cozy
chat. This way, Count Dracula. (*She hurries up the
Left stairs, trying for a youthful sprint and arrives at
the landing short of breath. She fans herself, turns to*
DRACULA *on the steps below.*) We'll go up in the elevator. (*A coquettish smile, her face half hidden by the
fan.*) Of course, sometimes it gets stuck. (*She exits.*)

DRACULA. (*Grimly.*) Not tonight! (*He exits after
her.*)

VAN HELSING. (*Waits a moment.*) Arthur, if you
will forgive me, I do not like your guest, Count Dracula.

SEWARD. Nor do I.

JONATHAN. That makes three of us!

VAN HELSING. Good. If we ever form a club, he
can't join. . . . Now, gentlemen, quickly, while we are
in trio we must talk of grave matters. Arthur, I assume
we take Mr. Harker into our confidence?

SEWARD. (*Nods.*) As Mina's fiance he has every
right to know.

VAN HELSING. Agreed. Please sit down, and try to

believe what I tell you. Your belief can save her life. (*Mystified,* JONATHAN *sits on sofa.* SEWARD *brings swivel chair down for* VAN HELSING.)

SEWARD. For you, Heinrich.

VAN HELSING. No, no. *Please!* (*Impatiently pushes swivel chair away.*) What I will say will make you unhappy, makes me unhappy—and when I am unhappy I pace. It is my safety valve. (*Waits till* SEWARD *is seated in desk chair.*) First, since I entered this house tonight, my worst suspicion has been confirmed.

JONATHAN. You mean that Mina—?

VAN HELSING. Please, young man. Facts first, questions afterward. (*Turns to* SEWARD.) Before I left Amsterdam I studied Wilhelmina's case history so often I could recite it to you from memory! Then I compared it, item by item, to the medical reports and coroner's report of the late Miss Lucy Westenra.

SEWARD. Coroner's report? How did you get that?

VAN HELSING. I sent an urgent cablegram from Holland. An unusual death can bring about a hasty marriage between medicine and the law—misalliance though it is. *You* know that, Arthur! . . . The similarity of Miss Westenra's symptoms to Mina's made me curious. More than that, they frightened me.

JONATHAN. Why?

VAN HELSING. Because Lucy Westenra had two little wounds on her throat—exact duplicates of those I found on Mina's throat! (*As both men start to rise he holds out his hands to stay them.*) Gentlemen, we are fighting no new disease here, no rare infection. We are fighting an enemy so powerful, so horrible you will deny his existence, but I tell you—with my heart's truth I tell you—Wilhelmina Murray is the victim of that creature, half human, half ghoul, called the Vampire. (*Both men are instantly on their feet in protest.*)

SEWARD. Good God, Heinrich!

JONATHAN. (*Overlapping* SEWARD.) Professor, you don't expect us to—

VAN HELSING. (*Tops them.*) Arthur! Mr. Harker! Please be still! . . . If you close your minds you are closing Mina's tomb.

JONATHAN. But you ask us to believe that Vampires are *real?* You ask us now, in the Twentieth Century, to accept superstition of the Dark Ages as fact? You ask too much! (*He turns away angrily, gets cigarette from his case, lights and inhales it deeply and moves up to the windows.*)

SEWARD. Heinrich, I know you well. I'm sure you mean every word, but—as one scientific man to another—what proof do you have?

JONATHAN. (*Coming down to them.*) He has no proof! How could he? Has he seen a Vampire suck blood from the neck of his victim? His whole theory is childish.

VAN HELSING. (*Quietly.*) In other words, I am in my second childhood.

JONATHAN. Vampires! Where do they exist but in Gothic novels, in pulp magazines, in superstitious minds of the ignorant? No living man has ever seen one— except when one is impersonated in a bad American movie. . . . I can't believe my ears. Mina is in danger and we talk of mythical creatures come back from the dead! (*He strides to bar, pours himself a shot and drinks it neat.*)

VAN HELSING. (*A pause, then to* SEWARD.) Arthur, the Westenra medical report states that the girl was given five massive blood transfusions.

SEWARD. Yes, Heinrich.

VAN HELSING. Yet she died of weakness, exhaustion. Where did all that healthy blood go?

SEWARD. We do not know.

VAN HELSING. Ah! You do not know! . . . Was there an open lesion through which it seeped away? No. . . . Did she have hemorrhages? No. . . . Did she have tiny wounds on her neck through which that blood could have been drained by a Vampire? *Yes!*

(JONATHAN *turns at bar, puts down his glass and listens.*)

SEWARD. But medical science—

VAN HELSING. (*Sharply.*) Medical science cannot explain her death! Yet you and science deny even the possibility of my theory because— (*Faces* JONATHAN *at bar.*) as you said, Mr. Harker, it is childish.

JONATHAN. (*Approaches* VAN HELSING *in amazement.*) You really believe what you're telling us, don't you? To you everything you say is perfectly sane.

VAN HELSING. Thank God, yes. Every word is based on the intelligence of an open mind and infinite research. I know the history, the horror, the incredible powers of the Vampire as no one else. Since boyhood he has been my hobby. My library is crammed with books on the occult, on necromancy, witchcraft, black magic, werewolves, vampires— Books that would astound you. These creatures—

SEWARD. We don't need books, Heinrich. You astound us.

VAN HELSING. All right, all right! I admit I never really believed. I half-believed, so I enjoyed my hobby. But tonight, with living evidence upstairs— (*Glances up Right stairway.*) that the Vampire *does exist,* does attack human beings, with that living proof surpassed by the dead proof of Lucy Westenra's bloodless body, tonight my hobby will help us save Mina's life.

JONATHAN. Us?

VAN HELSING. (*Stopped short.*) You will not help me?

JONATHAN. (*Quietly.*) I do not believe you.

VAN HELSING. Arthur? (SEWARD *cannot answer. He shakes his head and moves away. A silence.* VAN HELSING *gets his luggage, mounts Right stairs to landing, then turns:*) I have the same old room, Arthur? (SEWARD *nods.*) I will beg Mina to tell me the truth. She lied because she is afraid to— (*Suddenly puts luggage down on landing. He begins by addressing them*

calmly, but he ends by excoriating them both.) Let me
tell you some truths. (*Coming part way down steps.*)
After I have gone upstairs, you will call them lies. You
will say Van Helsing has gone insane.

SEWARD. My dear friend, don't—

VAN HELSING. Be seated and be *silent!* (*He waits.
To humor him,* SEWARD *sits again in swivel chair,* JON-
ATHAN *on tuffet below desk. When they are settled,*
VAN HELSING *slowly comes down into the room.*) I
want to shock your complacent, prejudiced minds! . . .
Vampires have the powers of the Devil. They can trans-
form themselves at will. A Vampire can come through
those windows or down that chimney as a bat and, in
the wink of an eye, assume human form. Or what appears to be human—for Vampires are the Undead,
corpses still half alive who roam the earth at night with
their insatiable thirst for human blood. (*Turns directly
to* JONATHAN.) Will you have more?

JONATHAN. I will listen.

VAN HELSING. By day the Vampire must return to
his coffin and lie helpless in daylight sleep, comatose till
sunset. Only by day is he vulnerable. Then, if you drive
a stake through his heart, you bring him ultimate death
and he crumbles to dust as you watch. But he can be
destroyed *only by day.* . . . At night nothing can harm
him. Night is his kingdom! . . . He can become invisible, so that you will not even know when one is beside you. He can appear in a fog, or dissolve in a mist.
How, then, can mankind fight him?

SEWARD. Heinrich, you are overwrought. You cannot
mean—

VAN HELSING. Overwrought? I am enraged by you
both! You will not let your eyes see nor your ears
hear. (*Apparently defeated, he crosses to Right stairway. Then he faces them again. His voice is quieter at
first, but it mounts with his conviction:*) One point
more; then I will go to Wilhelmina. . . . The Vampire
has fangs where we have the two canine teeth. These—

(*Indicates his own canine teeth with two fingers.*)
Fangs of needle point sharpness which are retractable
like those of pit vipers—the rattlesnake, the adder, the
copperhead. If you are unfortunate enough to witness
the Vampire's attack upon a human throat, you will see
those fangs. You can watch the incision, the opening of
the two tiny wounds—here! (*With the same two fingers
he presses the base of his throat.*) But you will never
witness that, gentlemen, because you are sensible men
who deny there are such creatures. . . . You and police
and public all deny him! . . . And it is that denial
which gives him his power. He has no enemies. Nothing
stops his heinous career because those who would fight
him are blind to his existence. . . . No, indeed, wise
men do not believe in Vampires! *Only fools believe—*
fools such as I. (*He turns, exits up Right stairs with
his luggage.*)

JONATHAN. (*Rising, he goes to stairs, looks up after
VAN HELSING.*) He meant every word. Dr. Seward, I
don't know what to think. *Is* he insane?

SEWARD. (*Rises, crosses Right to him.*) No. We all
have little quirks, obsessions. Now we know Professor
Van Helsing's obsession is the topic of Vampires.

(RENFIELD *enters quietly down Left stairway, sees
them and stops in fright. Then he realizes they are
unaware of him. Grinning, he scuttles to his fireplace stool and sits, highly pleased with himself and
suppressing his laughter.*)

JONATHAN. (*During RENFIELD's entrance.*) There
were moments when he almost convinced me. In a way,
I want to believe him. No matter what, I want to know
what is wrong with Mina! (RENFIELD *breaks with
maniacal laughter and they turn to him, startled.*)

RENFIELD. (*Rocking on his stool.*) You don't believe! You don't believe, but I am mad and I believe!

SEWARD. (*Goes to him quickly.*) Renfield! How did
you get here?

RENFIELD. (*Darts away to Left of desk.*) I came in a balloon! I sailed through the window on the wings of a giant bat! I was borne here on the back of Pegasus! (*Then, conversationally.*) How else would you enter a room?

JONATHAN. Doctor, who—?

SEWARD. He's a patient and he can be dangerous. Pull that bell cord for Hennessey. I'll buzz for the other attendants. (JONATHAN *pulls bell cord Right of fireplace. As* SEWARD *reaches for buzzer button on desk,* RENFIELD *puts his cupped palm over it.*)

RENFIELD. Don't ring for the others. Hennessey, yes. I hate all the others! They laugh at me. But then, I laugh at myself. (*Another burst of wild laughter which he stops short as he sees "housefly" above food tray. His eyes, his head follow the fly's flight.*)

JONATHAN. What—what is it? What does he see?

RENFIELD. A fly. A fat, juicy fly! (*Slowly raises cupped palm, catches "fly" and eats it with insane glee.*)

JONATHAN. (*Sickened, turns away.*) Good God!

RENFIELD. Where there's one there should be others. (*He wanders Left, looking for flies.* SEWARD *pushes buzzer button.* RENFIELD *drops to his knees, crawls on all fours below desk to Up Center, looks up at* SEWARD:) This place is too clean, Doctor. I never can find any roaches. (*He crawls behind swivel chair upstage.*)

HENNESSEY. (*Enters down Left stairs.*) Yes, Doctor?

SEWARD. It's Renfield. He's broken loose again.

HENNESSEY. Sorry, sir. I didn't know. I was in the dining room and—

WESLEY. (*Runs on from Down Right.*) Renfield? Have you got him?

RENFIELD. (*Pokes head up from behind swivel chair, sing-songs:*) Peek-a-boo! I-see-you! (WESLEY *and* HENNESSEY *close in from each side, take his arms.*) Please! Not so tight, my friendly keepers. I'm calm. I'll go quietly.

WESLEY. We've been looking for you for twenty minutes.

SEWARD. Why didn't the alarm go off?

WESLEY. (*Abashed.*) He cut the wires, sir.

SEWARD. Renfield, however did you get from your room to this side of the building?

RENFIELD. (*Rationally.*) It was an interesting trip. I slipped out of my room—that's always easy— (*Grins at both attendants.*) got out on the fire escape, stepped onto the ledge—

SEWARD. The ledge?

RENFIELD. Yes, and walked on the ledge all the way round the building. (*Makes a sweeping arc with one arm from extreme Right to Left over audience.*)

SEWARD. But that ledge is barely six inches wide!

RENFIELD. Exactly. That's what made it so exciting! I could have dropped to my death any minute. When I got to this side, I crawled up the drainpipe—

HENNESSEY. Crawled *up?*

RENFIELD. I'm a human-fly, you know. I got to the roof, came down those little circular stairs and here I am. It was simple—and your sister's on the roof. Somebody should watch her.

SEWARD. She's quite all right. She's with a guest.

RENFIELD. No, she's alone.

(SOUND: *DOGS HOWLING in distance.*)

SEWARD. Alone? She couldn't be.

RENFIELD. (*Shrugs.*) Very well, Doctor. Have it your way. (SOUND: *DOGS HOWLING UP LOUDER. Immediatly* RENFIELD's *calm is gone. He is in a frenzy.*) Listen! They know! They know what's going to happen. He'll be here—you cannot keep him out—and one of you will die! (*Wildly, pointing from one to another.*) But which one? Will it be you? Or you—or *you*—or *YOU?*

SEWARD. Hennessey, Wesley, take him away. (*They*

lead RENFIELD *toward Down Right. Except for his demented laughter, he seems cooperative. Then his body goes limp and he starts screaming.*)

RENFIELD. Master! Master, they are going to kill me!

(SOUND: *DOGS HOWLING UP TO CRESCENDO. As* ATTENDANTS *literally drag* RENFIELD *off Down Right,* SEWARD *closes French windows, draws gauze curtains shut and closes heavy draperies over them.* SOUND: *The HOWLING is muffled as windows close and FADES OUT during the following dialogue:*)

SEWARD. There! That will shut out that infernal howling.

JONATHAN. (*Looking Right after* RENFIELD.) Doctor, how do you stand it?

SEWARD. (*Leaving windows.*) The dogs? Oh, that's only a recent development within the last month. I've no idea whose they are nor what starts their howling.

JONATHAN. No, I mean how do you keep your own sanity when surrounded by the insane?

SEWARD. Oh, they're not all as bad as Renfield. Many are placid. Only a few are violent. (SYBIL *appears, somewhat distrait, on Left stairs and starts down, her ostrich feather fan folded and drooping at her side.*) Where is Count Dracula?

SYBIL. He's gone.

SEWARD. Gone?

SYBIL. Well, temporarily. He disappeared.

JONATHAN. (*A quick look at* SEWARD.) Miss Seward, you don't mean he fell off the—?

SYBIL. Oh, no. I was in the middle of a sentence and he just vanished! Right before my eyes.

SEWARD. That's impossible.

SYBIL. That's what I told him, but since he'd already vanished he didn't hear me. (*Sits disconsolately on sofa.*) I think it was rather rude.

(HENNESSEY *enters from Down Right carrying a small set of dinner chimes on mahogany frame with a felt-wrapped mallet.*)

HENNESSEY. Miss Seward, I brought you the dinner chimes. I thought you might like to summon everyone to the table.

SEWARD. In a moment, Hennessey. We'll wait till Miss Mina is down. (HENNESSEY *nods, starts for Left stairway with chimes.*)

VAN HELSING. (*Who has entered on Right stairway.*) That should be in five minutes or less.

JONATHAN. Professor, did Mina tell you—

VAN HELSING. The truth? Partially.

SYBIL. Wait, Hennessey. Let me hear those chimes. (*Hurries Left to him.* HENNESSEY *strikes chimes in sequence.*) Why, how dulcet! You've had them *tuned!*

HENNESSEY. (*Baffled.*) Er—yes, Miss. (*He exits into Left hall.*)

SYBIL. (*Mounting Left steps.*) Aren't they melodious? They've quite restored my spirits. . . . Arthur, what will we do about Count Dracula?

SEWARD. We'll start dinner without him.

SYBIL. I'm really very angry with him. I think I'll go unroll his napkin. (*Exits at top of Left stairs. Left to themselves,* VAN HELSING, SEWARD *and* JONATHAN *eye each other uncomfortably.*)

VAN HELSING. (*At last.*) Arthur, Mr. Harker, forgive my outburst. I am not sorry for what I said; I'm sorry I said it so loudly.

SEWARD. You must forgive us, too, but Jonathan and I were not prepared for your terrifying diagnosis.

JONATHAN. Please, what did Mina tell you?

VAN HELSING. Not enough. She admitted only that she is afraid to go to sleep. Night after night, she wakes from a nightmare with her heart pounding—she's gasping for air, her nostrils filled with a choking, sulphurous odor.

JONATHAN. God! What can it be?

VAN HELSING. I have *told* you, but you will not believe. She said it is always the same nightmare—of a large bat beating at her bedroom window. Then the window is blown open in a blast of cold air, her room fills with fog and mist and the great bat flies in, growing larger and larger, his blood red eyes staring at her. Then his noxious body covers her, smothers her—and she wakes screaming!

JONATHAN. Poor Mina. (*Turns to* SEWARD.) Doctor, is there a sedative—

VAN HELSING. Sedatives won't help—because her nightmare is not a dream, but reality.

SEWARD. But, Heinrich—!

VAN HELSING. One moment. (*Holding hand up for silence, he goes to Right stairs, looks up.*) I hear her coming. Say nothing, you understand? Nothing to alarm her.

(*All three face the stairs as* MINA *appears on the landing with a chiffon scarf hiding her throat. She descends in silence, hardly seeing them. On bottom steps she wavers.*)

JONATHAN. (*Hurries to her.*) Darling, are you sure you feel like going in to dinner?

MINA. I'm all right, Jonathan. Just tired.

SYBIL. (*Enters on Left landing with chime set at the ready.*) Dinner is served. . . . Oh, Mina, you're down. Splendid! I didn't think you'd make it. . . . Come along. . . . Everyone hurry before the Mock Turtle soup gets murky. (*She exits Left, striking the chimes, followed by* VAN HELSING.)

SEWARD. (*Waits politely.*) Mina?

MINA. Please, go ahead. We'll follow. (DR. SEWARD *exits up Left stairs.*)

JONATHAN. Take my arm, darling. We'll go in together.

MINA. Jonathan, I can't go in. I can't sit across the table from Professor Van Helsing.

JONATHAN. Why not, Mina?

MINA. He'll ask me more questions. Upstairs he made me tell him things I didn't want to.

JONATHAN. (*Cautiously.*) About your illness?

MINA. That and my loss of sleep and my terrible dreams and— (*Suddenly takes his hand, clutches it tightly.*) Jonathan, for the first time since her death, last night I dreamed of Lucy Westenra. I dreamed that Lucy was sitting on the edge of my bed. She looked so *real*, Jonathan. So *alive*, not a ghost. It frightened me. . . . She said she had come back from the grave to warn me that—that— (*Breaks off.*)

JONATHAN. Warn you of what?

MINA. (*A long look at him.*) I don't remember. (*Leaves him abruptly.*) No, I won't go in there. I can't face the concern for me in Dr. Seward's eyes, Sybil's inane chatter, the Professor's—

JONATHAN. (*Follows, hugs her close.*) All right, love. We'll have dinner in here. They won't mind. Besides, it will give us a little time together. Would you like that?

MINA. Oh, Jon, it would be heaven!

JONATHAN. (*Whips handkerchief from breast pocket, drapes it over arm like a waiter's napkin.*) This way, Madame! One heavenly dinner for two. Will Madame be seated? (*Seats her center of sofa and they both laugh.*) And next—our private dining table. (*Brings bench from fireplace, sets it below sofa.*) Now, lean your head back. Be lazy. Let me pamper you. (*Kisses her on the brow, starts out Left.*)

MINA. How lovely to be pampered.

JONATHAN. I'll go get our plates. (*Stops on Left steps.*) Do you mind if we skip the soup? I hate Mock Turtle.

MINA. (*Through a small yawn.*) So do I.

JONATHAN. Good. I'll wait and bring us the main course.

MINA. Jonathan, I'm very drowsy. And my eyes hurt so. (*Closes her eyes.*)

JONATHAN. Poor darling. I'll turn out the lights. Where's the switch?

MINA. By the bookcase.

JONATHAN. I see it. (*He flips wall switch by Left bookcase and ALL LIGHTS GO OFF except coals in fireplace and the dim light on the stairs at each side of the room. JONATHAN returns, kneels on sofa, kisses MINA gently.*) I love you.

MINA. (*Sleepily.*) And I love you.

JONATHAN. (*Goes up Left steps, stops on landing, whispers:*) More than life. (*She does not stir. JONATHAN exits Left.*)

(*The FIRELIGHT FLICKERS, then BRIGHTENS and MINA's head is silhouetted in a red glow. SOUND: WOLVES BEGIN HOWLING in distance. MUSIC UP softly, The Dracula Leitmotif. Then animal howling is augmented by WHISTLING OF THE WIND. Slowly the heavy DRAPERIES at French windows open by themselves. Then, just as slowly, the GAUZE CURTAINS open unaided. ANIMAL HOWLS fade out, topped by WIND reaching its peak as both FRENCH WINDOWS ARE BLOWN OPEN into the room. WIND dies down, MUSIC continues as HEAVY FOG seeps in through open windows. As MUSIC reaches a crescendo, a LARGE BLACK BAT flies in through windows, over MINA's head and disappears behind stone column at base of Right stairway. Immediately a FLASH POT goes off in the fireplace and COUNT DRACULA appears as though by magic, having leapt from "jumping platform" concealed behind Right column. Instantly a WOMAN USHER, at rear of auditorium, lets loose a blood curdling scream, joined, let's hope, by screams from women spectators. MINA stirs in her sleep. Her head rolls to one side. DRACULA slowly moves to behind sofa, unties her chiffon scarf, slides it from under her neck, tosses it into the air and watches it float to the floor. He bares his teeth in a hideous grin and his two fangs are plainly visible. With slow deliberation he bends over MINA, his lips working as he nears her throat. MINA wakes with a start, sees him above her and pushes herself away, screaming in terror.)*

MINA. Jonathan! Jonathan! *(DRACULA whirls upstage of sofa, his back to her. His cape and high collar cover his action from the audience as he removes and pockets the trick fangs. MINA, still screaming, backs away from him to base of Right stairs. JONATHAN races down Left stairway, flicking wall switch on the way. STAGE LIGHTS UP FULL.)*

JONATHAN. Mina, darling! What is it? What happened? *(As JONATHAN starts Right toward her, DRACULA turns, comes swiftly Down Center and intercepts him.)*

DRACULA. *(Smiling blandly.)* It is nothing, Mr. Harker. She was frightened by a bat. *(He crosses to MINA, fixing her with a steady, hypnotic gaze. She sways, steadies herself, and her expression becomes that of one in a trance. DRACULA links her arm through his, leads her toward Left stairs.)* Come, Miss Murray. Allow me to escort you in to dinner. *(JONATHAN watches bewildered as they pass before him and exit up the steps. He stands motionless, looking front, then dread realization comes to his eyes:)*

JONATHAN. *(Mouths the words silently.)* A bat! A bat! *(He is turning slowly, looking Left in DRACULA'S wake as—)*

(THE LIGHTS FADE.)

CURTAIN

ACT TWO

Scene: *The same.*

Time: *Nearly midnight, three nights later.*

At Rise: *The draperies and curtains at windows are closed. ALL LIGHTS ON and fire burns in the grate.* Jonathan, *in business suit, dignified tie and shirt, stands Left of desk with telephone in hand.*

Jonathan. Yes, Fred. . . . I know it's been three days, but what can I do? She's in grave danger. . . . I hate leaving you there in London to run the office alone. It isn't fair, I know, but— What's that? . . . Well, how can I predict? I *hope* I'll be back in a day or two— (Sybil *appears on landing of Right stairs, bifocals bobbing from the bosom as she descends. Her choice of evening gown is even less fortunate than before. She sees* Jonathan *at the phone and, in an effort not to disturb him, tiptoes to the Right of desk.* Jonathan's *phone conversation has continued throughout her entrance.*) No, I can't tell you exactly what's wrong with Mina. It's complicated and you wouldn't beli— What? . . . For God's sake, Fred, she's my fiancee! I love her and I'm trying to help save her life! . . . Yes, of course I sound terrified! A friend of hers died from this damnable thing. A young woman named Lucy—Lucy—

Sybil. (*A helpful whisper.*) Westenra.

Jonathan. Specialist? . . . Fred, this is beyond ordinary specialists. We're waiting now for Professor Van Helsing to get back from Amsterdam. He's our last hope. (Sybil *leans across desk, reaches for box of chocolates just beyond phone's base. Her wrist touches button of phone's cradle and disconnects the call.*) Hello?

50

. . . Hello! . . . Fred, are you there? . . . Damn! Miss Seward, you cut us off. (*Clicks receiver*)

SYBIL. Oh, dear. Did I?

JONATHAN. I'm afraid you did. Your arm pressed the cut-off button and— (*Clicking receiver insistently.*)

SYBIL. It could have been Operator doing it deliberately. They're very mean nowadays. (*Opens candy box.*) Have a chocolate?

JONATHAN. I can't even get Operator! Damn! These trunk lines from the country to London are hopeless. (*Slams phone into cradle.*)

SYBIL. When I want to reach London, I use postal cards. They're more dependable. (JONATHAN *glares at her, starts to reply, gets cigarette from desk box instead and lights up angrily.* SYBIL *wanders Right, munching a bonbon.*) Was it important?

JONATHAN. Just my business partner.

(DR. SEWARD, *in subdued sports jacket and dark trousers, comes on from Down Right.*)

SEWARD. (*As he enters.*) They still can't find Renfield. He's been missing over an hour. I don't see how he— (*Sees* SYBIL.) Why are you down here?

SYBIL. I just ran down for a chocky. (*Extends candy box.*) Have one?

SEWARD. No, I will not have one and will you please get back upstairs to Mina's room? It is urgent that someone be with her.

SYBIL. Why, Arthur? She's sound asleep and perfectly safe.

SEWARD. She is not perfectly safe. It's vital that she's guarded against attack.

SYBIL. Attack? By whom? (*The men exchange a look.*)

JONATHAN. I think you should tell her.

SEWARD. (*Desperately, under his breath.*) I can't. She would never—

SYBIL. Why can't you? And don't lower your voice. For three days you've all been behaving mysteriously. *And* for three nights, taking turns on guard by Mina's bed. Last night, when I fell asleep sitting beside her, I don't see why you were so angry. Nothing happened to her.

JONATHAN. Oh, God, if that were only true! I should have stayed with her till dawn.

SEWARD. But we have to spell each other, Jonathan. You can't go entirely without sleep. You cannot stay awake three nights in succession. That's seventy-two hours.

JONATHAN. (*Sits on tuffet, head in hands.*) Doctor, explain to her how critical it is.

SYBIL. Yes, Arthur, tell me. (*Sits on sofa, poking chocolates.*) I don't like being left out of things. Oh, tut! Somebody's eaten the last raspberry cream. (*Puts bifocals on, searches again.*)

SEWARD. (*Gets her to her feet, leads her toward Right stairway.*) Sybil, later when Mina is well, I can explain fully, but for the moment we know—Professor Van Helsing has proved to us—that under no circumstances must Count Dracula see Mina again. He— (*Looks to* JONATHAN *for help; gets none.*) His influence over her is—dangerous. Now, go sit beside her. I'll send Hennessey along shortly to relieve you.

SYBIL. (*A martyr mounting the steps.*) Very well, just as you say.

SEWARD. Whatever you do, don't unlock her windows. They must be kept fastened.

SYBIL. All right, but it makes the room awfully stuffy. That's why I get sleepy. (*Pauses on landing to test another chocolate.*) I can't understand Count Dracula's interest in Mina. He's old enough to be her father. (*She exits above.*)

SEWARD. (*Sighs, goes to* JONATHAN.) Everything goes wrong at once, doesn't it? I should have known we couldn't depend on Sybil—and Van Helsing's two hours overdue—and then, there's Renfield. He's been missing since ten o'clock.

JONATHAN. (*Looks up.*) How does he escape so often? Since I arrived here it's been—how many times?

SEWARD. I lose count. It's incredible, as though he had supernatural powers.

JONATHAN. (*Slowly rises. They look at each other.*) Are you thinking—?

SEWARD. Yes. I'm sure we have the same thought.

JONATHAN. There must be some connection, but how? And why? (*The TELEPHONE RINGS. SEWARD and JONATHAN move toward it simultaneously.*) Let me get it, sir. It may be my partner. He called before, but we had a little interference. (*Lifts receiver.*) Hello? Jonathan Harker here. . . . You want Dr. Sewa— Oh, Professor Van Helsing! . . . Where are you? We've been worried. (*As SEWARD reaches for phone HENNESSEY runs on from Down Right.*)

SEWARD. Let me speak to him.

HENNESSEY. Doctor, they found Renfield. He was—

SEWARD. One moment, Hennessey. (*To JONATHAN.*) Does Heinrich want me? Is he on his way?

JONATHAN. Wait a second, Professor. (*Lowers receiver.*) His car broke down. He walked five miles to the village. . . . Professor, we'll come get you. Where are you? . . . The pub? . . . The Lion and the Crown. Right. Be there in two shakes. (*Hangs up.*) Come on, Doctor, ride to the village with me. We'll pick him up.

SEWARD. I'd like to, but Mina—alone with Sybil? I don't know. . . . Hennessey, will you keep watch? We'll be gone just a short while.

HENNESSEY. Gladly. But about Renfield, sir?

SEWARD. Oh, yes. You say they got him?

HENNESSEY. Clayton and Wesley found him, all the way across the valley at Castle Carfax.

JONATHAN. Count Dracula's castle?

HENNESSEY. Yes, sir. Renfield was beating on the door, they said, shouting "Master! Master, let me in!"

SEWARD. (*Turns to* JONATHAN *slowly.*) We were right. There is a connection.

HENNESSEY. He sprang the lock on his own door, so we're putting him in a different room.

JONATHAN. (*Curbing impatience.*) Dr. Seward, the Professor is *waiting.*

SEWARD. Right you are. . . . Hennessey, put Wesley in charge of the wards. And you sit just inside Mina's room where you can keep an eye on her.

HENNESSEY. Yes, Doctor. I'll ring for Wesley. (*Goes to desk, pushes buzzer button.*)

SEWARD. (*Following.*) My sister is currently on watch, but she is apt to—to—

HENNESSEY. (*Tactfully.*) I understand, sir. Soon as I speak to Wesley I'll go right up.

SEWARD. (*Pats his shoulder.*) You're a good man, Hennessey. Without you this place would fall apart.

HENNESSEY (*Smiles, embarrassed.*) I'll ring again, sir. He must be in his quarters.

SEWARD. Well, Jonathan, let's go. (JONATHAN *hurries up Left stairs followed by* SEWARD. *As they exit above Left,* WESLEY *comes in from Down Right.*)

WESLEY. (*As he enters.*) You buzzed twice, didn't you? I was stretched out, catching my breath after that chase across the valley.

HENNESSEY. Take over the wards, will you, Wesley? I'll be upstairs keeping watch on Miss Murray while the Doctor's out. . . . Renfield locked up tight?

WESLEY. We put him in 14-A. He'll never break out of there.

HENNESSEY. I wouldn't bet. And the key?

WESLEY. Safe. Right here. (*From jacket pocket produces key with easily identifiable red tag, holds it up.*)

HENNESSEY. (*Mounting Right stairs.*) Good. Tidy up a bit here, will you? Use that tray from the bar.

WESLEY. Righto! (*Slips key into pocket, heads for bar.*)

HENNESSEY. (*From landing, calls upstairs.*) Miss Seward, I'll take over. Wouldn't you like to go back to your own room?

SYBIL. (*Off Right upstairs.*) Oh, splendid! (HEN-NESSEY *exits above.*)

(WESLEY *gets bar tray, collects used glasses from end table, one from mantel, others from desk, empties ashtrays, etc. As he returns to bar with tray, his back is to the windows. Window draperies are suddenly,* violently flung back *and* COUNT DRACULA *stands there, holding drapery edges at arms' length, his cape spread wide behind him like the wings of an enormous bat. He is in his immaculate white tie and tails and wears, as well, an evil smile.* DRACULA *steps forward and the draperies fall back into place behind him.*)

(PRODUCTION NOTE: French windows must be on two-way hinges. In Act One they have opened inward only; in Act Two it is necessary that they open outward onto balcony as well for stage effects later on. Thus, for his sudden appearance, Dracula got into position behind draperies without disturbing them since windows were pulled outward.)

DRACULA. Good evening. (WESLEY *turns, gasps, backs away fast to Left corner of bar, too frightened to yell.* DRACULA *goes to him. His tone is silken.*) I startled you, didn't I?

WESLEY. (*Whimpering in terror.*) Lord! Oh, Lord! (*As* DRACULA *approaches,* WESLEY *backs away with* DRACULA *following to Down Center. There, with a quick movement,* DRACULA *steps below him, all but blotting him from view with his cape.*)

DRACULA. Don't be alarmed. I'm Dr. Seward's

neighbor—from across the valley. (*Steps away from* WESLEY, *turns front, pocketing a small unseen object.*)

WESLEY. (*Stammering.*) Then you—you must be— be Count—Count—

DRACULA. Correct.

WESLEY. S-sorry, s-sir. I was a b-b-bit startled.

DRACULA. Evidently. The good Doctor is away?

WESLEY. Yes. Yes, sir.

DRACULA. (*Relishing the word.*) How *unfortunate.* Will you ask his ubiquitous sister if she will see Count Dracula? (SOUND: *At the mention of his name, DOGS BEGIN HOWLING in distance.* WESLEY, *repeating* DRACULA'S *name over and over like a litany under his breath, runs up Right stairs and exits.* DRACULA *smiles, holds up the key with red tag, then slips it back into a vest pocket. DOGS HOWLING GROWS LOUDER.* DRACULA *turns, gestures toward WINDOW DRAPERIES which OPEN at his silent command. Another gesture and GAUZE CURTAINS OPEN and finally FRENCH WINDOWS OPEN OUTWARD of their own accord. As windows open WIND sends gauze curtains billowing into the room. Across the valley we see Castle Carfax again and its tallest tower is dark. DOGS HOWLING GROWS LOUDER STILL.* DRACULA *goes to window and looks out. Calls toward his castle.*) Yes, yes, I hear you. Your howling is music, a dirge for the damned! For Mina— who soon will be one of us! (*HOWLING INCREASES and* DRACULA *laughs.*) That's it! Yelp your approval for the evil I shall do this night. Yowl and whine your derision for the fools who would stop me, the little men who will try to protect her. Mina shall die—and, in death, be my bride forever in the world of the Undead! (WESLEY *races down Right steps and, without breaking stride, moves rapidly Down Right.*)

WESLEY. Miss Seward's coming, sir.

DRACULA. Of course she is coming. I willed her to come.

WESLEY. Yes, sir. Anything you say, sir! (*Runs out Down Right.*)

(DRACULA *turns to balcony again, raises one hand. Immediately the HOWLING STOPS, the WIND DIES and the billowing CURTAINS FALL INTO PLACE and hang motionless.* SYBIL *descends Right stairs.*)

DRACULA (*Coming downstage.*) Ah, Miss Seward! A vision, as always.

SYBIL. Good evening, Count Dracula. I'm afraid you can't see Mina tonight. She's—she's indisposed and— (*Pleased with a sudden inspiration.*) still dreadfully despondent over her friend Lucy's death, so—

DRACULA. Ah, yes. Lucy Westenra. (*Straight faced.*) We had a passing acquaintance.

SYBIL. Well, Dr. Seward said Mina was not to be disturbed.

DRACULA. Dear lady, I did not come to see Miss Murray. (*Bows over her hand, kisses it.*) I came to see you! (*Leads her to swivel chair, seats her with a lordly flourish.*) In fact, I have brought you a gift.

SYBIL. A gift? How exciting. (DRACULA *steps above her and behind swivel chair, produces small, bright gold locket on slender chain from his vest pocket, holds it out just beyond her face.* SYBIL *starts to put on bifocals, but vanity prevails. She squints near-sightedly at the locket.*) A gold locket? How old fashioned. I mean—how lovely!

DRACULA. It has been in my family for generations. I want you to have it. See how it shines, how it catches the firelight. (*He sways it gently before her face. Unwittingly,* SYBIL *becomes a spectator at a tennis match. Her eyes follow the locket from left to right, her head turns slightly from side to side as the gleaming gold swings before her.* DRACULA'S *voice becomes softer, intimate, almost caressing.*) Long ago, whatever gold-

smith made it had you in mind. It was created to adorn
your lovely throat.

SYBIL. (*Eyelids growing heavy.*) Oh, Count Dracula,
I don't know how to—

DRACULA. (*Still swaying locket.*) Sh-h-h! Do not
speak. You are tired. You must rest. Close your eyes
and sleep. (*Whispering.*) Sleep. S-l-e-e-p. (*Her eyes
close, her head droops and falls forward. DRACULA
smiles malevolently, pockets the locket, spins the swivel
chair so that she faces him. He cups her chin, lifts her
inert head so that it lolls over the chair back. His voice
no longer caresses.*) You are asleep and yet awake.
Your subconscious receives and remembers every word
I say. . . . But you will not remember tonight's en-
counter. I have not been here. You have not seen me.
Do you understand?

SYBIL. (*Tonelessly.*) I understand.

DRACULA. You are now a menial, my servant, and
will do whatever I demand.

SYBIL. (*Monotonously as a parrot.*) Whatever-you-
demand. Whatever-you-demand. (*DRACULA spins swivel
chair in a half circle so SYBIL is facing audience. Her
expression is blank, her eyes unseeing.*)

DRACULA. Stand up! (*SYBIL rises.*) You will now go
to the wards, release the patient Renfield and bring him
here. . . . The key. (*DRACULA gives her the key. She
takes a few steps Right, holding key before her with its
tag dangling. Then she stops.*) Ah, yes. I read your
mind. You fear you will be seen by the attendants. Forget them. They are idling in their quarters. Go! Bring
Renfield to me! (*SYBIL continues her way and exits
Down Right. DRACULA laughs exultantly. A gust of
WIND billows the curtains again and DRACULA goes
to windows, looks up at the night sky.*) Ah, the night,
the night! Would that the sun never shone, that night
would last forever! (SOUND: *LOW MOURNFUL
HOWLING OF DOGS in the distance.*) That's right,
my ravenous, slathering friends. You agree with me.

(*Then, a gesture of dismissal.*) Enough. Begone!
(SOUND: *HOWLING DIES AWAY*. DRACULA *goes
swiftly up Right stairs to landing, looks up toward second floor. Then, apparently from the air, he produces
the long chiffon scarf* MINA *wore at the end of Act One.
Descending steps, he kisses it, fondles it, tucks it into
inner pocket. Once more he causes a flaming cigarette
to appear from nowhere, blows out the flame and is
smoking lazily when* SYBIL *enters Down Right leading*
RENFIELD *by the hand.*) Well done. You will make an
excellent servant.

RENFIELD. Master, she—

DRACULA. Silence! She must know nothing. (*Approaches* SYBIL.) When this hypnotic state has passed,
you will recall nothing that has transpired.

SYBIL. (*An automaton.*) Nothing that has transpired.

DRACULA. But when again I need you, your mind,
your will are powerless to resist me. Repeat that.

SYBIL. My mind, my will are powerless to resist you.
(DRACULA *laughs, joined by* RENFIELD *who is silenced
by an imperious gesture.*)

DRACULA. (*To* SYBIL.) Go to your room. (*She obediently starts to Right staircase.*) No! That will not do.
(*She stops.*) Hennessey is upstairs. He must not see
you hypnotized. Let me consider. (*In thought, and not
seeming to notice, he puts burning cigarette into his
loosely closed hand as though extinguishing it. When he
opens the hand, the cigarette has vanished.*) Go instead
to your music room. (SYBIL *turns, starts Left.*) Devote
your addled brain to the scores of Bach, Purcell, Handel. Confound your minuscule intelligence with their
hemi-demi-semi-quavers. (SYBIL *mounts Left stairs at
sleepwalker's pace and exits.* DRACULA *turns sharply to*
RENFIELD *who crumples to his knees.*) Now, you! I
have work for you.

RENFIELD. Master, I thought you had renounced me.
I ran through the valley, beat on your door, but you
would not let me in.

DRACULA. With two men at your heels? The risk **was** too great. Would you have them learn too much?

RENFIELD. No, Master. Never!

DRACULA. Listen and obey me. (*Pulls him to his feet.*) You will go upstairs and conceal yourself until Mina is unprotected. Then you will burst into her room, threaten to kill her—

RENFIELD. Oh, Master, no! I beg you—

DRACULA. Be silent and *hear me!* . . . You will frighten her so thoroughly that she will ask her guardian, her lover, and that damnable Dutchman to let her sleep here. The fools will let her. Their tiny minds will not conceive that here she will be more—*accessible* to me.

RENFIELD. Hide myself? Up there? I've never been upstairs. (*Scuttles to his stool and sits bunched up, quivering.*)

DRACULA. Think of it as an adventure. Consider! You shall also commit your first theft.

RENFIELD. Theft?

DRACULA. (*Amused at* RENFIELD's *fright.*) Exactly. You have read your "Oliver Twist"?

RENFIELD. I—I think so, when I was little—

DRACULA. Momentarily, I am your Fagin. Once you have terrified Mina, it is my will that Van Helsing and Dr. Seward shall come to seize you. In the struggle, you will steal their crucifixes.

RENFIELD. (*Puzzled.*) They have crucifixes?

DRACULA. They will, shortly. Tonight each will receive one from Van Helsing—that devotee of Vampire lore. He knows I cannot touch nor look upon a crucifix. He knows too much to live long. . . . The sanctimonious cowards will wear their godly artifacts here— (*Indicating his breast pocket.*) over their hearts. In the melee, as they remove you from Mina's room, you will relieve both Doctor and Professor of their holy burdens.

RENFIELD. And Mr. Harker's crucifix?

DRACULA. Later. I have my own plans for the heroic Mr. Harker. When the three simpletons reach for their crucifixes to stay me— (*Begins to laugh.*) Without them, they will be helpless!

RENFIELD. Oh, Master, I cannot! To attack Miss Mina, who has always been kind to me— Please, I beg you—!

DRACULA. (*Approaching him.*) Think of it in terms of reward. You shall have fat flies to eat, plump spiders, small succulent chipmunks and, ultimately—if you do well—your first taste of human blood!

RENFIELD. (*Ecstatic, rocks on stool.*) Blood! "The blood is the life!" It says so in the Bible.

DRACULA. (*Casually.*) I've yet to read it. (*He moves away.*)

RENFIELD. (*Rises, follows him.*) But Hennessey is up there. He will see me.

DRACULA. Hennessey is a simple man, simple to control. He will not hinder you. I shall hypnotize him.

RENFIELD. (*Amazed.*) From *here,* Master?

DRACULA. From *anywhere!* You do not know my powers. Never doubt me. Never question. You are to obey. Nothing more. (*MUSIC BEGINS The Dracula Leitmotif.*) Should you not obey, the punishment is death! (*MUSIC SURGES.*)

(*COMPLETE BLACKOUT including fire in the grate. DRACULA exits through secret panel in Right wall. This should require five seconds or less, a span filled by RENFIELD'S cry in the dark:*)

RENFIELD. (*In blackout.*) Master! Master, where are you? (*LIGHTS UP FULL INSTANTLY. MUSIC DIES. A sudden HIGH WIND blows the CURTAINS again. RENFIELD, searching wildly for DRACULA, looks up as a LARGE BLACK BAT flies from top of Right column, through the windows and out of sight. He runs after it out onto balcony.*) I shall do as you command, Master. I shall obey you.

(WIND subsides, CURTAINS are still. Jabbering to himself, RENFIELD runs up Right stairs, then hesitates on the landing. MEN'S VOICES off Left startle him and he dashes on up, exits above. JONATHAN enters Left carrying VAN HELSING'S old Gladstone bag, followed by VAN HELSING holding a good sized cardboard carton wrapped with brown paper and heavy twine. VAN HELSING wears another suit just as rumpled as its predecessor. Last to enter is DR. SEWARD.)

VAN HELSING. Drop that Gladstone anywhere. This can go on the desk. *(Puts carton on desk's Left end.)*
SEWARD. Shall we help you open it?
VAN HELSING. Later, later. It all goes into your laboratory. I have something else to show you first. . . . We have much to do this night. May we have coffee?
SEWARD. Excellent idea. I'll ring for Hennessey.
JONATHAN. Doctor, Hennessey is guarding Mina.
SEWARD. How stupid of me. I forgot. . . . Buzz for Wesley, will you, Jonathan? Three shorts and a long.
VAN HELSING. I'm glad *someone* is guarding her after your telling me what happened last night. You said this morning the two little wounds were freshly opened and irritated?
JONATHAN. *(Pressing desk buzzer.)* Yes, and she's weaker than ever.
VAN HELSING. He got to her again. There's no doubt of it.
JONATHAN. Oh, God! If only I'd been there. *(Bitterly, to VAN HELSING.)* Miss Seward slept through it all!
VAN HELSING. We cannot be sure of that.
SEWARD. What do you mean?
VAN HELSING. She may have been mesmerized. *(His manner becomes business-like.)* But that's behind us. It is Mina's welfare this moment that is important. Aside

from her weakness and the freshly opened wounds, is she otherwise—different?

JONATHAN. (*On guard.*) Different?

VAN HELSING. In my absence have you noticed any change in Mina's personality?

JONATHAN. (*Quickly.*) No!

SEWARD. Yes. (VAN HELSING *looks from one to the other for explanation.*)

JONATHAN. (*Defeated.*) Yes, we have.

SEWARD. An alarming change. In these last three days she's begun to behave oddly. Sometimes, without warning, she will turn on us as though she hated us.

JONATHAN. And, just as suddenly, she will become amorous. It's not like Mina to be demonstrative.

VAN HELSING. I expected it. As she falls further under the Vampire's spell, the change will be more marked each day. Finally she'll become a stranger you'll not recognize.

JONATHAN. I can't believe that.

VAN HELSING. In time, you will. . . . By chance have you found her looking at herself in the mirror, rubbing the mirror's surface, then staring at her reflection again?

SEWARD. No. Why?

VAN HELSING. It is one more sign that— (*He stops as* WESLEY *enters Down Right and crosses to* SEWARD.)

WESLEY. Sorry not to have been quicker, sir. I was with Dr. Grayson.

VAN HELSING. (*To the others.*) I'll explain later.

SEWARD. Wesley, make us some coffee, will you? A large pot. We'll be up quite late.

WESLEY. Glad to, sir. (*Starts out, then remembers.*) Oh, Doctor, while you were out Miss Seward had a visitor. He—

SEWARD. Not now, Wesley. We're busy.

WESLEY. Yes, sir. (*Exits Down Right.*)

VAN HELSING. Gentlemen, sit down. I have a news item, from *The Times*, no less. (*Draws swivel chair near sofa, sits, pulls folded* London Times *from jacket pocket.*) I just happened on it while dining in London.

JONATHAN. Professor, can't that wait? What you said about the mirror—

VAN HELSING. No, this cannot wait.

JONATHAN. But, Mina—!

VAN HELSING. This article could well be Mina's story —if she dies before we stop Count Dracula.

JONATHAN. Stop?

VAN HELSING. Destroy! (*Shakes paper open, begins reading.*) "20th August, 1934, Purfleet."

SEWARD. (*Surprised.*) That's this township.

VAN HELSING. Exactly. "Elusive Young Woman Continues Attacks on Small Children. . . . A series of strange attacks on small children has baffled local officers of the law. Yesterday agents from Scotland Yard joined Constable Bradley and his men in a round-the-clock-search for the mysterious, beautiful young woman who is often seen, but never apprehended, with local children at twilight and in the early evening. The little victims, interviewed at Purfleet Hospital, say she gives them candy, walks with them through the woods, kisses and fondles them, and then disappears in a kind of mist."

JONATHAN. (*Repeats quietly.*) In a kind of mist.

VAN HELSING. (*Nods, continues reading.*) "Children examined by physicians have been slightly torn or wounded in the throat. The wounds are tiny, two little white dots with red centers, such as might be made by a rat or small dog. No adult has seen this young woman except from a distance. Police have nothing to go on but descriptions given by the youngsters, each of whom says she has long, rippling red hair and a slight limp in the left foot." (DR. SEWARD *gives a cry of horror and looks at* VAN HELSING. *Silently,* VAN HELSING *folds* The Times, *rises, puts it on desk.*)

JONATHAN. What has that to do with Mina?

VAN HELSING. Ask Dr. Seward. He knows.

SEWARD. (*Rises, goes to* VAN HELSING.) I can't believe it.

VAN HELSING. The evidence is irrefutable. She had long red hair, did she not? And the pathological report mentions a deformity of the left foot, sufficient to cause a limp.

JONATHAN. (*Rises.*) Who? Who?

SEWARD. Lucy Westenra.

VAN HELSING. (*Triumphantly.*) *Yes!*

JONATHAN. But she's dead!

VAN HELSING. Not truly dead. She is one of the Undead, a Vampire created by Dracula. He killed her; now she is one with him, a ravening, blood hungry creature of the night.

JONATHAN. My God, how horrible. And Mina—?

VAN HELSING. Unless we kill Count Dracula *now*, before he kills Mina, she is doomed to the same fate—to become a bestial thing, half human, half carnivore. (JONATHAN *covers his eyes, moves away upstage.*) We must trap him here, hold him here till daybreak when he is powerless. Then we destroy him! Either that, or hunt him down by day in his coffin. Logic says that coffin must be somewhere in his castle.

JONATHAN. (*Goes to window, looks at castle.*) Let's go there now. We'll wait there for him till dawn. I'll get a tree branch, a fence rail, *anything* to make a sharp wooden stake—and *I* will drive it through his heart!

VAN HELSING. (*Crossing to desk.*) I have brought a stake. It is in this box with devices to make him our captive. (*With pocket penknife he cuts twine away from carton.*)

SEWARD. Heinrich, how can he be trapped without escaping us?

VAN HELSING. One step at a time, Arthur. First, we three believe he will come again tonight. Agreed?

JONATHAN. (*Coming down from window.*) Agreed.

VAN HELSING. You see that his castle tower is dark. That means he's waiting out there somewhere in the night. (*Rips wrapping paper away from carton.*) By now his craving for Mina's blood is insatiable. More than that, he wants her dead, to be with him, to share the horror of his half-life. . . . Mina is our lure— (*Lifts spray of blue and white blossoms from carton.*) these will prevent his getting near her.

SEWARD. How?

JONATHAN. What are they?

VAN HELSING. Blossoms of the Batswort, a plant that grows only a few places on earth. It flourishes in Holland. It was primarily for these flowers that I went back to Amsterdam.

JONATHAN. But how—? What does it—?

VAN HELSING. It is Nature's way to fight the Vampire. Vampires cannot stand the sight, the smell nor the touch of Batswort. It is an anathema to them. They run from it as we would flee the Bubonic Plague. . . . A garland of these blossoms, worn like a necklace by Mina in her sleep, will keep Count Dracula at bay.

SEWARD. Heinrich, you are sure?

VAN HELSING. Please! Don't start to lose faith now. Have I not been right about Vampires up to this point?

JONATHAN. Yes, Professor. We'll do anything you say. We've *got* to believe you. You're our last hope.

VAN HELSING. (*Smiles ruefully.*) I like to win, but not by default. Believe in me because you want to.

JONATHAN. (*Offering his hand.*) I want to.

VAN HELSING. Good. There are other things Vampires abhor. Religious articles, for example— (*Takes small crucifix on chain from carton.*) a small crucifix, any replica of the sacred cross terrifies them. I have four of these, one for Mina and one for each of us. (*He beckons them closer and hands a crucifix to each.*) Take them. We will need them and the power of good they represent before this night is over. Keep them with you —here. (*Indicates his breast pocket. Each puts his crucifix in breast pocket.*) Now, in this box are other repellents to deal with Vampires; Hawksweed, Aconite, Monkshood and Deadly Nightshade which—

(*A terror stricken SCREAM from* MINA, *upstairs off Right, freezes all three where they stand. Another SCREAM and they realize its source. They run to Right steps,* JONATHAN *in the lead. Before they can start up,* MINA *runs down the stairs and straight into* JONATHAN'S *arms in a state of hysteria. Sobbing, she tries to tell them what is wrong, but she is incoherent. Her hair hangs loose, she is in a beautiful low-cut floor-length nightgown. Over it she wears a soft, flowing negligee and in one hand she clutches a long handled, silver backed hairbrush. The three men get her to the sofa and seat her,* JONATHAN *beside her with his arms about her comfortingly.*)

JONATHAN. Darling! Dearest Mina, you're safe now, safe with me. Don't cry, darling. Don't cry.

VAN HELSING. Was it Count Dracula? (*Still sobbing,* MINA *can only shake her head.*)

SEWARD. (*Goes to Right stairs, calls up.*) Hennessey! Hennessey, what's wrong up there? (*He waits.*) That's odd. He can't be asleep, not with Mina screaming so. *Hennessey!*

MINA. (*Between sobs.*) Don't—call him. He couldn't —help—me. He's—in—a trance.

VAN HELSING. Hypnotized! It *was* Dracula!

MINA. No, no! It was—Renfield.

SEWARD. (*Astounded.*) Renfield? In your room?

MINA. (*Slowly recovering.*) Yes. He—he was hiding in my closet. When I opened it he leapt at me in a frenzy. I've never—never seen him so violent. I tried to—to fight him off with my hairbrush and—

JONATHAN. Did he hurt you?

MINA. No, but he frightened me horribly. He kept saying over and over, "The Master is coming to drink your blood! The Master is coming to—"

VAN HELSING. Where is he now?

MINA. Still in my room. I ran into the hall and locked the door behind me. He's in there with Hennessey.

SEWARD. Hennessey? Hypnotized and can't defend himself! God help us, Renfield will kill him. Heinrich, quick! Jonathan, you stay with Mina. (SEWARD *and* VAN HELSING *run up Right stairs and exit.*)

JONATHAN. Poor darling. What a terrible fright you've had. (*Kisses her gently on the cheek.*)

MINA. Jonathan, I will not stay in that room again. I'll sleep down here. (*Looks around the room.*) It's more open here. I'll not be cornered like a trapped animal again. You can guard me just as well here.

JONATHAN. Of course we can. Better, in fact. (*Goes to French windows, examines the locks.*) And these windows can be fastened just as tightly against the Count as those in your bedroom.

(*While* JONATHAN *is upstage of her, a strange GREEN LIGHT suffuses* MINA *on sofa. MUSIC: A lone, haunting THEREMIN BEGINS The Dracula Leitmotif.* MINA *sits up gradually, languidly begins brushing her hair, looking over the sofa's back at* JONATHAN. *He is out on balcony, checking windows. As* MINA *speaks, the THEREMIN MUSIC FADES AWAY.*)

MINA. (*Strangely seductive.*) Jonathan?

JONATHAN. (*Still busy.*) Yes, Mina?

MINA. Come give me a kiss.

JONATHAN. In a minute, dear. (*Looks up, grins.*) I did kiss you, not thirty seconds ago.

MINA. (*Leans back on sofa, arms wide across its top, enticingly.*) I mean a real kiss, not a peck.

JONATHAN. (*Interested, starts toward her.*) Oh, you do? (*Stops.*) Mina, I don't think this is exactly the moment nor the right spot—

MINA. You're so proper. What's the matter with you?

JONATHAN. What's the matter with *you?* I've never seen you like this before.

MINA. Perhaps you've never looked.

JONATHAN. (*Lightly.*) Oh, come off it. I know you by heart, head to toe.

MINA. (*A low, provocative laugh.*) Jonathan, do me a favor. Bring me that small mirror from the hall console. I want to brush my hair.

JONATHAN. (*Smiles.*) Oh, women! Who can figure them? A minute ago you were in hysterics, now you want to look romantic. (*Starts up Left stairs.*)

MINA. (*Rises, moves toward him.*) Well, if I'm going to seduce you, I must look my best.

JONATHAN. (*Half seriously.*) Mina! What a thing to say! (JONATHAN *exits Left.* MINA *crosses up to windows, looks out.*)

MINA. Castle Carfax. He has never invited me there. I wonder what it's like? (*She comes down toward desk, notices Batswort blossoms in carton, lifts them out. Then her face contorts with revulsion and she drops them quickly on the floor, backs away.*) What a horrible odor! Revolting! (JONATHAN *enters Left with oval shaped boudoir mirror, small pier glass type, on its own stand and which can be tilted.*)

JONATHAN. Here's your mirror, darling.

MINA. Thank you, love. Put it on the desk and, Jonathan—would you move that strange box of weeds and things? It has a dreadful odor.

JONATHAN. (*Puts mirror on desk, gets carton.*) Really? I hadn't noticed. (*He goes Up Right, puts carton on fireplace bench.* MINA *sits at desk, adjusts the tilt of the mirror, barely glancing into it, and begins brushing her hair with slow, deliberate strokes, all the while eyeing* JONATHAN.)

MINA. Come do this for me, won't you? I adore to have someone brush my hair, especially my lover.

JONATHAN. (*Smiling, going to her.*) I think "fiance" is the more respectable term.

MINA. Who wants to be respectable? (*She gives him the brush and leans back invitingly.* JONATHAN *brushes her hair.* WESLEY *enters Down Right bearing tray with china coffee pot, cups, saucers, etc. He takes it to bar.*)

WESLEY. Here's the coffee, Mr. Harker. Feeling better, Miss Mina?

MINA. I *never* felt better! (*As* WESLEY *starts to leave,* SEWARD *and* VAN HELSING *enter down Right stairs holding a subdued* RENFIELD *between them.*)

SEWARD. Don't go, Wesley. Give us a hand with Renfield. Hennessey's not well enough to help. (*To* JONATHAN *and* MINA.) It took us forever to find Renfield. He was curled up in a ball on the top shelf of your closet, Mina.

MINA. (*Laughs aloud.*) How very amusing. (VAN HELSING *gives her a sharp look, releases* RENFIELD'S *arm so* WESLEY *can take hold.*)

WESLEY. (*To* SEWARD.) I can handle him alone, sir.

SEWARD. Too risky. We'll stay together till he's locked up.

RENFIELD. I can walk by myself, thank you, if you'll unhand me.

WESLEY. Not a chance! That's how you got away from me last time.

RENFIELD. And I'll do it again, you fool! And again —and *again*—and *AGAIN!*

MINA. (*Reaching for hairbrush.*) That's enough, Jonathan. (*Fondles his hand.*)

VAN HELSING. (*Picking up blossoms.*) How did these flowers get on the floor?

MINA. (*Coolly.*) I tossed them there. They have a dreadful smell. (VAN HELSING *studies her again, but she is unaware of it. She has turned to the mirror and is gazing at her reflection, puzzled.*)

WESLEY. (*Crossing Down Right with* RENFIELD *and* SEWARD.) I don't know what happened to the key for

14-A, Doctor. It just vanished from my pocket. Where will we put him this time?

SEWARD. Considering his violence toward Mina, we'll make it solitary confinement.

RENFIELD. (*Plants both feet, with mounting frenzy.*) Solitary? You think that will hold me? The Master will set me free. Free! Locks and bolts and bars won't stop him. He will release me and then—he has promised me —a feast of blood! (*Screaming.*) "The blood is the life! The blood is the life!" (SEWARD *and* WESLEY *manage to get* RENFIELD *out Down Right and the screams die away.*)

MINA. Jonathan, look. The strangest thing. My face is blurred in the mirror.

JONATHAN. Maybe the mirror is dusty.

MINA. (*Rubs her hand across it, examines her palm.*) No. Bend over. There, you see? Your face is perfectly clear—and mine is blurred. How very odd. (VAN HELSING *moves near desk, looks into mirror obliquely and gives a little gasp.*) What did you say, Professor?

VAN HELSING. (*Moves away.*) Nothing.

JONATHAN Never mind, darling, blurred or clear, you're ravishing.

MINA. Then give me a kiss, a real kiss!

JONATHAN. Gladly! (*As he bends to kiss her,* VAN HELSING *swiftly moves in, holds his crucifix between their faces. With an animal's snarl,* MINA *springs to her feet and backs from them.*)

MINA. Damn you! Damn you! (*Suddenly she bursts into tears, sinks onto sofa, hiding her face.*)

JONATHAN. (*Starts to her.*) Darling! What is it?

VAN HELSING. (*Grabs his arm.*) Don't touch her till she is herself again.

JONATHAN. Why? What's wrong?

VAN HELSING. Already the change in her is dangerous. Her blurred face in the mirror is proof. By tomorrow her likeness there will disappear entirely.

JONATHAN. What do you mean?

VAN HELSING. Vampires cast no reflection. (*Putting crucifix in pocket.*) Thank God I still had this. Upstairs Renfield tried to— (*He stops as the spectral GREEN LIGHT FADES from around* MINA. *She looks up at* JONATHAN *tearfully, once more herself.*)

MINA. My darling, forgive me. You must never kiss me again. I am unclean, a foul thing no man should love.

JONATHAN. Mina, dear, don't say such things.

MINA. You don't know, you don't know! Last night when he came to me—

VAN HELSING. While Sybil slept in her chair?

MINA. She wasn't asleep. He looked at her with those horrible red eyes—they are red at times, like a vulture's—and she was paralyzed.

VAN HELSING. Mesmerism! Just as I thought.

JONATHAN. And you? Mina, what did he do to you?

MINA. (*Weeping again.*) He—he forced me to— He opened a vein in his chest—and—forced me to drink his blood! He held me tight in a loathsome embrace with my mouth pressed to his bosom—so that I must swallow or strangle! Then he called me his bride. . . . Oh, Jonathan, Jonathan! I wish I were dead!

JONATHAN. (*Sits quickly, holds her close.*) No, no! Don't say that. (*He looks pleadingly at* VAN HELSING *over her shoulder.*)

VAN HELSING. We have to work fast. It must be done tonight. And *here!* (DR. SEWARD *returns from Down Right. At the same time,* HENNESSEY *starts carefully down the Right stairway rubbing his brow.*)

HENNESSEY. Dr. Seward, I'm sorry. I don't know what happened. I must have blacked out.

SEWARD. It's all right, Hennessey. How are you now?

HENNESSEY. Not well, sir. I have the most blinding headache.

SEWARD. Better go to your room. Wesley can look after things.

HENNESSEY. Thank you, sir. Miss Mina, I'm sorry I failed you. (*He exits Down Right.*)

VAN HELSING. (*Lifts his carton from fire bench.*) Arthur, Jonathan, we three will now go to the laboratory.

SEWARD. Yes, Heinrich. I'll bring the coffee. (*Gets coffee tray from bar.*)

JONATHAN. (*Still soothing MINA on sofa.*) Dr. Seward, Mina is afraid to stay in her room. She'd rather sleep down here tonight.

SEWARD. (*To VAN HELSING.*) Is it safe?

VAN HELSING. We must make it safe. Come along. Time was never more precious. (*Crosses to desk with carton.*)

JONATHAN. (*Getting up.*) But who will stay with Mina?

MINA. (*Drying her eyes.*) Don't worry. I'm all right now. (*Unnoticed by the others, VAN HELSING puts carton on desk, takes several sprays of flowers up to the windows.*)

SEWARD. (*Puts coffee tray down.*) No, you must not be alone. Hennessey is ill, Wesley is taking charge for him, and—and—

JONATHAN. Isn't there any other attendant you trust?

SEWARD. They all have their hands full in the wards.

(*By now VAN HELSING has closed French windows and is busily rubbing the seams, edges, locks and handles with flowers. SYBIL appears on Left stair landing. She seems herself again, but one hand is pressed to her brow and she descends the stairs with great care. Each step makes her wince.*)

SYBIL. (*An echo of HENNESSEY.*) I have the most blinding headache.

VAN HELSING. (*Looks round briefly from his work.*) You, too?

SYBIL. And I can't remember what happened tonight.

(*Sinks into swivel chair.*) My mind is absolutely vacant!

SEWARD. Heinrich, what are you doing?

VAN HELSING. Rubbing the juice of the Batswort flowers around these windows. As long as they are not opened again, the odor will linger and keep the Vampire away. And here, my dear— (*Takes a garland of flowers from carton, goes to* MINA.) Wear these blossoms around your neck to ward him off. And this— (*Gets crucifix on chain from pocket.*) this will stop him if all else fails. (*He puts crucifix, then garland about* MINA's *neck, then closes curtains and draperies.*)

MINA. What pretty little flowers—and their fragrance is so delicate.

JONATHAN. You said they were horrible.

MINA. Did I? I don't remember.

SEWARD. You swear they will protect her? Nothing can happen?

VAN HELSING. He will not touch them, nor touch her—as long as she wears them. Now, let's go. Quickly.

JONATHAN. (*As* SEWARD *starts to pick up coffee tray again.*) I'll take that, sir. (VAN HELSING *exits first up Left stairs carrying his carton, followed by* JONATHAN *with coffee tray.* SEWARD, *last to leave, turns on landing to* SYBIL.)

SEWARD. Sybil, whether you keep awake or fall asleep, stay with Mina. Just for comfort's sake.

SYBIL. I don't feel well enough to do anything but stay. I've absolutely taken root in this swivel.

SEWARD. (*Drily.*) It's possible. (*He exits above Left.*)

SYBIL. It's frightfully peculiar. It's as though I'd been asleep and waked up to find myself in the music room thumbing through Bach's B Minor Mass.

MINA. Sybil, dear, do you mind if we don't talk? I'm very tired and would like to rest.

SYBIL. (*Seriously.*) Oh, I wasn't talking. I was just

thinking out loud. (*Presses both hands to her temples.*) Dear me, how my head aches!

MINA. (*Stretches out on sofa, head at Right end.*) You should rest, too. Why don't you go upstairs? I'm perfectly safe now.

SYBIL. After while. At the moment, the slightest movement might be fatal. (MINA *settles more comfortably, closes her eyes and turns her head away from the audience.*)

(*MUSIC BEGINS SOFTLY, The Dracula Leitmotif, and LIGHTS SLOWLY FADE leaving only the fire's glow and offstage hall lights. As the music starts, SYBIL lowers her hands from her temples and looks front. Gradually the large PAINTING ON SCRIM above fireplace mantel IS ILLUMINATED FROM BEHIND. DRACULA becomes visible through the painting and he beckons. SYBIL rises slowly and approaches the now transparent painting. DRACULA holds up the gold locket and chain he used earlier and gently sways it back and forth. As before, SYBIL's head moves with it and she is hypnotized. The MUSIC, ghostly, heavily minor and lugubrious, CONTINUES UNDER ACTION until just after the next blackout.*)

DRACULA. (*Softly.*) You are now receptive to my will.

SYBIL. (*Tonelessly.*) What is your command?

(DRACULA *holds finger to his lips for silence, puts locket away, raises one hand, closes fingers as though around a hanging cord, then his hand slowly descends as if pulling a drawstring. SYBIL nods, moves to the windows in a dream, opens the draperies by their drawstring, then the gauze curtains. DRACULA pantomimes again, bringing both hands forward as though grasping two doorknobs, then separates hands in a slowly widening gesture*)

*of opening two portals. SYBIL nods, opens the
French windows out onto balcony. He gestures toward sofa and SYBIL dreamily moves down to it.
DRACULA mimes removing garland from MINA'S
neck. SYBIL leans over sofa back, breaks garland
in half and slips it from under MINA'S head, lays
what is now a string of flowers over sofa back.
DRACULA now points to his chest, puts lower halves
of arms together to form a cross, turning his face
away in disgust. SYBIL gently lifts the sleeping
MINA'S head, removes crucifix and chain from her
neck. DRACULA smiles in cruel triumph, pantomimes dropping two lightweight objects, one from
each hand. SYBIL nods again and with crucifix in
one hand, she picks up the string of blossoms with
the other. DRACULA slowly disappears as LIGHTS
BEHIND SCRIM FADE OUT and STAGE
LIGHTS COME UP. SYBIL goes to balcony and
drops garland and crucifix over the rail. During
this DRACULA comes down from backstage platform behind scrim, gets in position behind secret
panel for his entrance in blackout. After SYBIL has
dropped the two articles, she moves trance-like
out of sight Left on balcony. A LONG, SUS-
TAINED OMINOUS CHORD and MINA wakes,
sits up, eyes wide, hands covering her throat as
though for protection. MUSIC SWELLS. FAST
BLACKOUT. In blackout DRACULA enters through
the secret panel and crouches low behind sofa, out
of audience sight line.)*

MINA. (*In blackout.*) Sybil? Sybil, where are you?
. . . Jonathan! (*LIGHTS DIM IN AGAIN TO
FULL. MUSIC OUT.*)

(*Dead silence. DRACULA'S hands appear over sofa back,
one at either side of MINA'S neck. Just as they are
about to close round her throat, MINA rises and
moves away from sofa to Down Right Center.*

DRACULA'S *head and shoulders now appear from behind sofa, then he stands completely, his* fangs *bared. He goes to* MINA, *tilts her head back and she collapses over his arm, head hanging back loosely, throat exposed. Again* DRACULA *bares his fangs, then lips and jaws are working as he lowers his head toward her throat.* SYBIL *returns on balcony from Left, moves Down Left Center rubbing her eyes, coming out of her trance.* DRACULA'S *back is to her and, to all appearances, having pierced* MINA'S *throat, he is too involved to notice* SYBIL. *But she notices him—in the midst of his blood-thirsty hobby.* SYBIL *screams at the top of her voice.* DRACULA *roars like a wild beast, quickly lays* MINA *on sofa and lunges toward* SYBIL. *She screams anew, backing away Down Left.*)

SYBIL. Help! Oh, help! Arthur! Arthur! Mr. Harker! *Help! HELP!* (MEN'S VOICES *and RUNNING FOOTSTEPS are heard off Left.*)

DRACULA. My curse upon you! (*As* JONATHAN, SEWARD *and* VAN HELSING *enter Left and race down the stairway—*DRACULA *runs toward the balcony.*)

SYBIL. Quick! The balcony! Count Dracula! He—!

(*The men rush shouting onto the balcony to catch him. Their three bodies in a tight row block audience view so that* DRACULA, *by ducking well below their shoulders, can exit unseen Left on balcony. At this same moment FLASH POT goes off in fireplace to divert audience attention. Further distraction comes from* SYBIL *who, frightened by flash pot, screams again and slumps in a dead faint Down Left. After flash pot and faint, a LARGE BLACK BAT sails in through window and flies directly downstage. The men rush forward in pursuit, looking up as BAT FLIES OUT OVER THE AUDIENCE and disappears at back of auditorium. THE LIGHTS FADE.*)

CURTAIN

ACT THREE

SCENE 1

SCENE: *The same.*

TIME: *Twenty-eight hours later, before dawn.*

PRODUCTION NOTES: *Oval standing mirror used in Act Two is now fastened to desk top and mirror's pivots tightened so glass will not tilt when it is smashed by* DRACULA. *Bell cord Right of fireplace is now rigged to come down with one quick yank by Renfield.*

AT RISE: *ALL LIGHTS UP FULL. Across the valley the TOWER LIGHT BURNS in Castle Carfax. French windows are open outward onto balcony, draperies and gauze curtains are open.* VAN HELSING *is seated on sofa smoking his pipe.* DR. SEWARD, *tie loosened, shirt collar open, is Left of bar holding an idle coffee cup.* JONATHAN *stands at the open windows facing the balcony, his back to the audience, his hands out of sight before him. He is tie-less with shirt sleeves rolled up. His necktie and jacket lie across sofa back, Right end. All three men are as motionless as figures in a frieze. Nothing moves except smoke curling from* VAN HELSING'S *pipe. The mood is one of quiescence, of sleepless fatigue. Then* JONATHAN *slowly raises one arm, his body shielding the action from the audience, and fires a pistol into the night. Instantly he leans over balcony rail and peers down.*

VAN HELSING. (*Brought to his feet by the shot.*) Great God!

SEWARD. (*Overlaps.*) Jonathan! (*Simultaneously there is a SCREAM upstairs off Right from* SYBIL.)

JONATHAN. (*Turns, pistol in hand.*) Sorry if I startled you.

SEWARD. *Startled* us?

VAN HELSING. What in hell— (*Another SCREAM from* SYBIL *and we hear her hysterical voice from the top of the Right stairs:*)

SYBIL. (*Off, upstairs.*) Was that a *shot?* What's the matter down there?

JONATHAN. (*Calls toward steps.*) It's all right, Miss Seward. Just some target practice.

SYBIL. (*Off.*) Scared me to death!

JONATHAN Everything's fine. Don't come down.

SYBIL. (*Off.*) Come down? I've got to *lie* down! I'm a wreck! (*Her whimpers die away above.*)

VAN HELSING. (*Still in shock.*) What target practice?

JONATHAN. I said that just to calm Sybil. I was shooting at a bat.

SEWARD. (*Astounded, to* VAN HELSING.) He was shooting at a—!

JONATHAN. I guess I wasn't thinking straight, but I was hoping that bat would be— (*Looks sheepishly at both.*) Crazy, wasn't it?

VAN HELSING. (*Begins to relax.*) Truthfully, yes. Even if the bat had been Dracula, no bullet would have killed him. At night Vampires are invincible.

JONATHAN. (*Fervently.*) So you told us, but I had to do something *positive* for a change! I'm sick of frustration, sick of this eternal waiting—waiting! Killing time waiting to kill him!

SEWARD. (*Goes to him.*) I know. We're all ready to explode.

VAN HELSING. The three of us are like walking volcanoes. But simmer down, Jonathan. (*Patting his shoulder.*) Bank your fire.

SEWARD. (*Indicates pistol, puzzled.*) Is that yours?

JONATHAN. No, it's yours. It was on the desk when I came in here alone. I picked it up and then— (*Gestures toward window, then hands pistol to* SEWARD.) I'm very sorry.

SEWARD. No, it's my fault. This is always locked up. I cleaned it tonight and then forgot. (*Takes keys from pocket, locks pistol in desk drawer.*) Risky to leave it out and available to my insane friends. (*A nod toward doorway Down Right.*)

JONATHAN. Including me?

SEWARD. (*Smiles.*) Not likely. (SEWARD *returns to his coffee at the bar,* VAN HELSING *ambles to fireplace puffing his pipe and* JONATHAN *goes back to French windows, holds curtain aside, looks out.*)

JONATHAN. (*After a silence.*) Not a sign. The light in his castle tower is still burning. God, how I wish it would go out. I want to know the exact minute he's on his way. (*Lets curtain fall back, comes downstage, looking at wristwatch.*) It's nearly 4:30 A.M. What if he doesn't come tonight?

VAN HELSING. He'll come. We kept him from Mina last night. Tonight he's bound to come. His appetite for her blood will drive him here.

JONATHAN. And if it doesn't?

VAN HELSING. We'll do exactly as we did yesterday; go to the castle after sunrise and search for him in his coffin.

JONATHAN. And pray to God we'll find him— (*Picks up sharp wooden stake from desk.*) and drive this into his heart! . . . How he must have smiled, like a grinning skull, as he lay there—*somewhere,* safely hidden in that coffin while we hunted for it. (*Slams stake back on desk.*) Five hours of futile search!

SEWARD. Jonathan, think of it as an exploratory foray. If we have to look for his crypt again, we'll benefit by that first search.

VAN HELSING. It has *got* to be a sort of secret vault, somewhere beneath the castle.

JONATHAN. But we went over that entire basement, like dedicated bloodhounds!

SEWARD. I never saw dust so thick in all my life.

VAN HELSING. Nor so many cobwebs.

JONATHAN. Did you notice? Not a sign of life in those cobwebs; only shriveled husks of dead spiders.

SEWARD. That whole experience was a shock. I'd never been inside the castle before. (*Glancing out the windows.*) Looking at it from here, it always seemed romantic. Mysterious. But to find it a shell of whatever glory it once had, its windows broken, its doors hanging from their hinges, not a stick of furniture in it. How does he live there?

VAN HELSING. (*Sits on sofa, settles back.*) He doesn't live there. He lives at night, abroad in the world. What need does he have for furniture, for a home? His home is that hellish coffin!

JONATHAN. Yes! If only we could find it! (*Goes to Right stairs, looks up.*) Mina's taking an awfully long time up there. She's on edge, like the rest of us. Can't sleep. I wish she could. She needs it.

SEWARD. So do we all. She'll be down shortly, Jonathan. She just went to get some sewing material. She said she must do something with her hands to keep her mind off— (*He stops. Both men wait a moment for him to finish, then* VAN HELSING *nods understandingly.*)

JONATHAN. (*Another look up the steps.*) I worry when she's out of my sight even for a minute.

VAN HELSING. Stop pacing. Sit down! She's all right. She's wearing a fresh garland of Batswort blossoms and her crucifix. I put both round her neck myself.

JONATHAN. Yes, she had them on night before last, remember? And Sybil removed them! (*Calls up the stairs.*) Mina?

MINA. (*Off, upstairs Right.*) Yes, Jonathan?

JONATHAN. What's keeping you, love?

MINA. (*Off.*) I'll be down—well, in a while. Sybil has lost her sewing basket.

JONATHAN. And?

MINA. (*Off.*) We're looking for it. It might take time. Sybil's forgotten what it looks like. Don't worry. I'm all right.

JONATHAN. (*Gives up, grins at the others.*) Women!

SEWARD. Well, at least she sounds quite herself.

VAN HELSING. (*Rising.*) Yes, but I've not told you. (*Crosses to desk, empties pipe into ashtray.*) She had a bad spell this afternoon. I was reading in here, right in this chair— (*Taps desk chair, then taps pipe against ashtray as they wait.*) and I looked up and found her behind me. She had crept in without a sound, like a cat. And that's the odd thing—her expression was feline, her eyes narrowed like an angry cat's, her fingers workings like claws. (*Puts pipe down to demonstrate contraction and expansion of fingers.*) She looked as though she were ready to spring at my throat and said, "You're trying to trap him, aren't you? Trap him with your silly herbs, your Batswort, your crucifixes. But you won't succeed. I shall warn him!" . . . Then, a minute later, she was herself again and remembered nothing at all.

JONATHAN. Mina said "I shall warn him"? Do you believe she would betray us?

VAN HELSING. The Wilhelmina you love would not, but the Wilhelmina she is becoming will be a dangerous enemy. If we don't kill the Vampire soon, the change in her will be irrevocable.

SEWARD. (*Hesitantly.*) Heinrich, you said that if Mina dies—before he dies, she will— (*He cannot finish.*)

VAN HELSING. She will become one of the Undead, a feeder upon human blood, a hellhag.

JONATHAN. (*To himself.*) Another Lucy Westenra.

(*Turns away.*) Oh God, my God! I don't think any man alive or all through history ever had an experience so horrible—to watch the woman he loves become a rapacious harpy right before his eyes. There are moments when I really think I'm losing my mind, that you'll have to put me in there, Dr. Seward— (*Looks toward Down Right.*) with the insane! (JONATHAN *moves above desk, his back to them.* VAN HELSING *gives* SEWARD *a nod and they go to him. At* VAN HELSING's *touch on his shoulder* JONATHAN *straightens up, but his voice is unsteady:*) Professor Van Helsing, Dr. Seward, to kill this demon, to save Mina, for that I swear I would sell my soul!

VAN HELSING. No. Only the Devil buys souls—and we are busy enough with him now. Sit down, my boy. (*Eases him into desk chair.*) Arthur, get him some coffee.

SEWARD. (*Starts up to bar.*) I'm afraid it's cold.

VAN HELSING. No matter. Hot or cold, he needs it. (*Takes cigarette from desk box, hands it to* JONATHAN, *lights it.*) Despair is one thing, Jonathan, lack of sleep is another. Right now all our hopes are clouded by fatigue, but believe me, our plan will work. It *must*.

JONATHAN. You're right. It's fatigue. I'm dead for sleep. (*Pillows his head on folded arms on the desk, burning cigarette still between his fingers. Then, a mumble:*) God, I'm tired. So tired.

(*Gently* VAN HELSING *takes cigarette from* JONATHAN's *fingers, crushes it out. As* SEWARD *approaches desk with coffee* HENNESSEY *enters Down Right in pajamas and bathrobe, carrying a tray with second coffee pot, cups, saucers, etc.*)

HENNESSEY. I brought fresh coffee, sir. Since you're staying up all night I had a hunch you'd need it.

SEWARD. It was a good hunch. Thank you, Hennessey. There'll be no sleep for us till daybreak.

HENNESSEY. Very little sleep in the asylum either, Doctor. Almost all of the patients are restless. There's a full moon and that always affects them, but tonight— I mean, this morning— (*Puts tray on bar, looks at watch.*) Good Lord, it's past 4:30. Well, they're more upset than usual; staring out their windows, pacing, some crying, some laughing at nothing. (*Takes used tray with cold coffee, etc., which* SEWARD *holds out to him.*)

SEWARD. (*Pouring fresh hot coffee for* JONATHAN.) And Renfield? He's locked up securely?

HENNESSEY. Still in solitary, sir. His second night. I think for once we've got him flummoxed. (*Starts Right with tray.*)

SEWARD. (*Carries fresh coffee to* JONATHAN *who's now asleep on desk, shakes him gently, then more firmly.*) Jonathan? . . . Jonathan! . . . Here, drink this. We've all got to stay awake.

JONATHAN (*Sits up, rubbing eyes.*) You mean I actually dozed off?

VAN HELSING. (*To* HENNESSEY.) Is Renfield up, too? Pacing, like the others?

HENNESSEY. Professor, he's worse than the others. Half hour ago I looked in on him and he was running back and forth, like a fox in a cage. He was sobbing and calling out "Master! Master!" and saying something about how the Master had deserted him. . . . That's sort of his pattern now, sir. His sleeping habits have changed. He naps during the day, stays awake most of the night. (*Starts out again toward Down Right. The three men look at each other.* JONATHAN *rises.*)

JONATHAN. Hennessey, wait a minute. (*Drinks coffee at a gulp.*) Dr. Seward, please, may we get Renfield in here? I swear we're right. There's a tie-in between him and Count Dracula. Maybe Renfield can tell us where the vault is, where that coffin is hidden. We know he's been to the castle—

HENNESSEY. Four times, sir.

SEWARD. I'm not sure we should.

VAN HELSING. Come now, Arthur!

SEWARD. It doesn't seem right, questioning a mental patient in the middle of the night, especially one as mad as he. If he's in one of his erratic moods, you'll get nothing from him.

VAN HELSING. Let's try. A few questions can't harm him and, God knows, it's in good cause. Jonathan's idea might be our Open Sesame to the vault.

SEWARD. (*After brief hesitation.*) I see I'm out-voted. All right, Hennessey. I'll come with you. (HENNESSEY *and* DR. SEWARD *exit Down Right.* VAN HELSING *goes to bar, pours himself coffee as—*)

(MINA *descends Right stairway still in nightgown and negligee and wearing the garland of Batswort flowers and crucifix round her neck. Over one arm she carries an evening gown, folded so that little of it shows, but the color is inescapable. She wears evening shoes rather than bedroom slippers.* SYBIL *clops down the stairs behind her in nightgown, robe and noisy slippers, her hair tortured into old fashioned paper curlers. She carries a small, wicker sewing basket with top. Unhappily the whole ensemble—the nightgown, robe, floppy bedroom shoes and paper curlers enhance* SYBIL *less than her outfits hitherto.*)

MINA. (*With amusement on her way down.*) We finally found Sybil's sewing basket. It was at the bottom of her laundry hamper.

SYBIL. (*On landing holds basket up in triumph, then wilts before their united steady gaze.*) Well, I have a solid gold thimble, you see, and I hide it from prowlers. Then I forget where.

JONATHAN. (*Meets* MINA *at foot of stairs.*) Darling, you look better. Your color's coming back.

MINA. Thanks to these— (*Touches garland.*) and the Professor's other talismans, Count Dracula hasn't been able to get to me for two wonderful, peaceful nights. I've had time to recuperate.

SYBIL. (*Descending stairs.*) While she's recuperating, I'm going into a decline. It's days since I've felt really tip-top.

VAN HELSING. Have some coffee.

SYBIL. Heavens, no. But I will have a drop of sherry. So many doctors recommend it. (*Hurries to bar, pours herself sherry from decanter.*)

JONATHAN. Coffee, Mina, dear?

MINA. No, thank you. I'm wide awake. Any stimulant would be redundant.

JONATHAN. I envy you. I'm asleep on my feet.

SYBIL. (*Accusingly to* JONATHAN.) You and your wicked target practice! I rarely drink sherry at 5 A.M.— (*Tosses it down.*) but I need this for my nerves. (*Pours herself another.*) Why are you both still dressed? Arthur, too, I remember. Isn't anybody in this house going to bed tonight?

JONATHAN. (*Joins her at bar, pours himself a second black coffee.*) We're waiting for Count Dracula to pay us a nocturnal visit.

SYBIL. That horrible man? I wouldn't let him in the door, now that we know what he's after! At first, I thought his interest in Mina was purely avuncular.

MINA. (*Sits on sofa, evening gown folded on her lap.*) It's ironic, Sybil, to hear you say you wouldn't let him in. Give me your sewing basket, please. It was you who first invited him here.

VAN HELSING. So it was you? . . . Interesting.

SYBIL. Why? (*Hands sewing basket to* MINA *over back of sofa.*) What do you mean?

VAN HELSING. It's interesting, Miss Seward, because one of the limitations of the Vampire's power—and there are *few* limitations—is that he may not enter a home unless he is first invited by someone who lives there. In this case, you! . . . Once he has gained entrance, he may come and go as he likes. (*They all look at her.* SYBIL *grows uncomfortable under this trio of stares.*)

SYBIL. Well, I was being neighborly. After all, he'd just moved in across the valley. I met him by chance one evening while on a short cut through the cemetery. He was most courteous. . . . I asked him if, as a newcomer, he had any friends here and he said no, no actual friends, just some close contacts. I felt sorry for him. Then I made the unfortunate mistake of inviting him to dinner. (*Finishes her sherry.*) Well, it all proves what mother said years ago; you should always have a formal introduction. (*Starts to bar for a refill.*)

JONATHAN. (*Puts cup and saucer down.*) There! Two cups of coffee, one for each eye. They're open again. . . . Is that a new dress you're working on, Mina? That color is very becoming to you.

MINA. (*Matching spools of thread to gown.*) I know. That's why I thought I'd alter it. It's not new, it's old and out of style. I'm going to raise the hem and plunge the neckline.

JONATHAN. (*Grinning.*) Careful! It's safer the other way round.

SYBIL. Well, you ply your needle, dear. That's your therapy. When I can't sleep I have to read. (*Goes to Left bookcase, puts bifocals on, scans book titles.* DR. SEWARD *and* HENNESSEY *bring* RENFIELD *in Down Right. He wears standard, colorless institutional pajamas and thin cotton robe. He is barefoot. He looks suspiciously at each one in the room.* SYBIL *greets him amiably from the bookcase:*) Good evening, Renfield. Why are you barefoot?

HENNESSEY. (*When* RENFIELD *doesn't answer.*) He threw his slippers out the window, Miss.

RENFIELD. (*Blurts it out.*) And my shoes. Shoes hamper me. With bare feet I get a prehensile grip.

SYBIL. (*Matter of fact.*) Of course you do. (*Goes back to her book titles.*)

SEWARD. (*Indicates fireplace stool.*) Would you like

to sit in your corner, Renfield? (*Without answering,* RENFIELD *scurries instead to tuffet below desk and sits hunched up, facing audience, glowering.* SEWARD *turns to* HENNESSEY.) Much appreciation, Hennessey. Now get back to bed, get some sleep.

HENNESSEY. Not yet, Doctor. I'd better stay up to keep an eye on the inmates. Most of the attendants are on alert, sir. We're all ready for trouble. (*He exits Down Right.*)

JONATHAN. (*Fast cross to* RENFIELD.) Now!

SEWARD. (*Catches his arm.*) Easy, Jonathan. You have to start this sort of thing in low gear.

JONATHAN. Of course. Sorry, Doctor.

VAN HELSING. I don't think we should start at all until— (*A gesture toward* MINA *and a significant nod.*)

SEWARD. Oh, yes. I see what you mean.

SYBIL. (*Crossing below them all to Right bookcase.*) Whatever you're doing, go right ahead. You won't bother me. (*Begins to check through book titles.*)

JONATHAN. (*Sotto voce.*) Which of us will tell her? (MINA *looks up from threading her needle. She does not turn to them but faces front with a little smile, addressing them all:*)

MINA. No one has to tell me anything. I know. You are going to question Renfield about Castle Carfax and it is better that I do not know what information you ask, nor his answers. (*All three men come downstage slowly, look at her wonderingly.*)

JONATHAN. How do you know?

VAN HELSING. Did you overhear us discuss this while you were upstairs?

MINA. No, Sybil and I were in the back of the house in her room, looking for this, remember? (*Holds up sewing basket.*)

JONATHAN. Then, darling, how—?

MINA. (*Smiles at him.*) I wish I could say it's as innocent as woman's intuition, but it's more than that.

Lately, I've been able to foresee things, to know what people will do, to read their minds. It—it really frightens me, Jonathan. Especially when it concerns Count Dracula. Not always, mind you, but I can anticipate his coming, know what he will say, what he is thinking. I read his mind the clearest of all.

VAN HELSING. (*After a silence, to the men.*) It is part of her becoming more and more—

MINA. (*Finishing it for him, rises.*) A Vampire. Yes. That's why it terrifies me, that and the fact that I never know when I shall turn on you suddenly, change into that detestable woman who says she hates you. You know that is not the real Mina. I could never hate you. (*Goes to them, giving each a gentle caress.*) I'm grateful to you for what you're doing, for trying to save me. I'm grateful and I love you— (*To* JONA- THAN.) Especially you, my darling. (*She begins to cry.* JONATHAN *takes her in his arms, leads her Left, away from the others.* RENFIELD *turns on the tuffet, faces* MINA.)

RENFIELD. (*Softly.*) Don't cry, pretty lady.

MINA. (*Drying her eyes, reaches out, pats* REN- FIELD'S *cheek.*) You're quite right, Renfield. I shouldn't cry. It doesn't help matters a bit. . . . Jonathan, dear, bring me my dress and Sybil's sewing basket, will you? (*As* JONATHAN *goes to sofa for them, she turns to* RENFIELD, *speaks quickly under her breath:*) Tell them everything you can, Renfield. Help us. Oh, *please,* help us!

RENFIELD. (*Turns away from her.*) No! I can't. I can't!

JONATHAN. Here you are, dear. (*He hands her the gown and sewing basket.*)

MINA. Come along, Sybil. The men want to talk without us.

SYBIL. (*Still at Right bookcase.*) Just a second. I've found something. (*Pulls out volume, checks cover.*) *Latin!* Wouldn't you know? (*Puts it back, takes an-*

other.) Dickens. Tsk, equally dry . . . "Dombey and Son." The very thing. Last time I read it, it put me to sleep! (*She starts Left toward* MINA. SEWARD *and* VAN HELSING *are in quiet conversation near fireplace.* MINA *and* JONATHAN *are part way up Left stairs and absorbed.* RENFIELD, *isolated on tuffet, is in his own nether world. Seeing she is unobserved,* SYBIL *detours to the bar, gets the sherry decanter, holds it up to see that it's half full, conceals it in the folds of her robe and aims for Left stairs, Dickens aloft in the other hand, addressing* MINA *en route:*) We'll go in the dining room. There's a good reading light, the table's big enough for you to spread out your gown at one end, and for me to put my head down and take a nap at the other—if Dickens lulls me as he used to. (*She sails past the couple on the stairs and exits Left.*)

JONATHAN. Be sure to keep that garland round your neck, *and* your crucifix!

MINA. Yes, love. (*She goes up to the landing, blows him a kiss and follows* SYBIL *off Left. The three men quietly approach* RENFIELD; VAN HELSING *above him,* JONATHAN *at his left,* SEWARD *at his right. Without shifting position on tuffet,* RENFIELD *throws his head back, turning it in an arc, taking in the three faces above him.*)

SEWARD. Renfield, you would like to help Miss Mina, wouldn't you?

RENFIELD. I would like to, but I can't. I dare not! (*Puts head down between knees, doubles over in a tight ball.*)

SEWARD. She needs your help badly. We all do.

RENFIELD. (*Suddenly slides from tuffet to his knees before* SEWARD.) And I need yours, Doctor. I implore you, let me out of this house. Send me away, anywhere where he can't find me. Send keepers with me with whips and chains! Manacle me! Put me in leg-irons! Send me to jail. Some place away from him so that, day by day, he will not get another little piece of my soul! (*Slumps to the floor, begins beating it with his fists.*)

SEWARD. We'll get nothing out of him when he's like this.

VAN HELSING. I'm afraid you're right. (RENFIELD *spreads out full length on the floor, face upstage, sobbing softly.*)

JONATHAN. It's hopeless? (*Sighs heavily as they nod agreement.*) One more door slammed shut! . . . Well, if you're sure he won't talk, I'll take a shower. Anything to wake me up. I'm falling asleep where I stand. (JONATHAN *starts up Right stairs, taking off his shirt, revealing T-shirt underneath.* RENFIELD *gets up from the floor and hurries to* SEWARD *and* VAN HELSING *who have moved Up Center.*)

RENFIELD. Dr. Seward! I'll help you. Why shouldn't I? If he abandons me, why should I be loyal? I'll tell you everything I know. (*This outburst stops* JONATHAN *on the landing. He,* SEWARD *and* VAN HELSING *look at each other, then hold motionless. None of them notices the castle TOWER LIGHT FLICKERING RAPIDLY. Now, as all four men hold still, it GOES OUT.* RENFIELD *begins pacing, eyes staring, not focusing on them as he speaks:*) For two nights I called his name, begged him to release me from that solitary cell —and he never answered. His promises to me were lies! All lies! (*Grabs* SEWARD *by the lapels.*) Listen. He said if I hid in Mina's room, attacked her, frightened her so that she would beg to sleep down here—he said I'd be rewarded, that I should have my first taste of human blood. A Saturnalia of blood, he called it. But he *lied!* Not a drop, not one tiny little drop! (*Flings himself onto sofa, arms wide, hands clutching cushions, head thrown back, eyes vacant.*)

JONATHAN. (*Descending steps, shirt over his arm.*) Renfield, I'm sorry he lied to you and—

RENFIELD. *He'll* be sorry! He'll be sorry, you'll see!

JONATHAN. Yes, I'm sure we will, but right now—

VAN HELSING. Jonathan, let me do this. I've had a bit more experience. (*Sits beside* RENFIELD, *takes his hand, pats it soothingly.*) Renfield, Count Dracula broke faith with you, didn't he? You hate him now, don't you?

RENFIELD. Yes, yes. (VAN HELSING *beckons to* SEWARD *who eases himself down onto sofa at* RENFIELD'S *other side.* JONATHAN *moves to above sofa, just behind them.*)

SEWARD. And you'd like to see him punished.

RENFIELD. Yes, yes! Tortured! Burned! Hanging by his thumbs!

VAN HELSING. Then help us punish him.

RENFIELD. (*Looks from one to the other rapturously.*) What sweet revenge! What can Renfield do to punish Count Dracula?

SEWARD. There is a vault in his castle where he sleeps by day in a coffin.

RENFIELD. I know. (*All three lean toward him.*) I've never seen it, but I know it's there.

VAN HELSING. (*Dismayed.*) You've never seen it?

RENFIELD. He never let me, but I know it's under— under—

JONATHAN. (*Impatiently, flings shirt down over sofa back.*) We know it's *under!* Where else would a vault be?

SEWARD AND VAN HELSING. (*Turn to* JONATHAN *together.*) Sh-hh!

VAN HELSING. (*To a small child.*) Tell us, Renfield, what is it under?

RENFIELD. (*After a long, brow furrowed pause.*) It's under—something. (*With a loud sigh of exasperation,* JONATHAN *turns away. He gets a warning signal from* VAN HELSING. RENFIELD *taps* SEWARD *on the shoulder:*) But I remember— (*Again all three strain toward him.*) once when I was in the castle basement with him, he disappeared through a secret—I mean it **was sudden, like magic, you know?** But I'm sure he went through a hidden— (*The WIND WHISTLES LOUDLY and the curtains blow into the room. All four turn toward the windows at the sound. Then, just as suddenly, the WIND DIES DOWN, the curtains are stilled and THICK FOG begins to roll into the room.* RENFIELD *leaps up, runs to windows, calling wildly:*) I did not betray you, Master. I did not say where it is hidden. They know nothing. Nothing! . . . I am your slave! I worship you. . . . Master? . . . Master, answer me! (*He waits. There is no reply. Only the FOG CONTINUES TO ROLL IN.* RENFIELD *screams in a paroxysm of terror:*) Oh, God! He will kill me. He will kill me! (*He runs to his stool by the fireplace, hunches down on it, hiding his face in the mantel corner.* VAN HELSING *rises, motions* SEWARD *and* JONATHAN *to follow him downstage away from* RENFIELD. *As he speaks the FOG THINS OUT AND EVAPORATES.*)

VAN HELSING. Dracula is here. I can sense it. He is invisible, but here, somewhere in this house! Remember? They can materialize out of a fog and disappear in a mist? . . . We must move fast before he gets to Mina. Arthur, hurry! Come help guard her!

SEWARD. (*As* VAN HELSING *pulls him toward Left stairs.*) Jonathan, quickly! Pull that bell cord. Tell Hennessey to put Renfield back in solitary. (VAN HELSING *and* SEWARD *run up Left stairway and exit.* JONATHAN *starts toward bell cord but* RENFIELD *gets there first.*)

RENFIELD. No! Not solitary. (*Begins laughing, low at first, then mounting into hysteria.*) You'll never put me back there! (*He rips bell cord from the wall with one powerful tug, balls it up, runs to balcony and throws it over the rail.* JONATHAN, *who tried to catch him, follows up stage, but stays at a safe distance still within the room, uncertain of* RENFIELD'S *next move.*) What good would it do? He'll find me—anywhere, and torture me to death. (*Comes down to* JONATHAN, *staring, babbling.*) No! He'll not kill me! I'll kill myself.

Yes, that's it. *Kill myself! Now!* (*He turns, runs to the balcony and throws one leg over the railing, but* JONATHAN *is fast enough to grab him before both legs are over. He lifts* RENFIELD *bodily from the rail, propels him back into the room and in an instant they are fighting. It's a whale of a fight that takes in the whole room. There are moments when* RENFIELD *breaks free and heads for the railing again, only to be caught and pulled back to safety. In the battle's course,* RENFIELD *rips* JONATHAN'S *T-shirt so that it hangs in shreds. Finally,* RENFIELD *trips* JONATHAN *who falls out of sight behind the sofa. With an exultant cry,* RENFIELD *grabs his wooden stool, lifts it high and is about to crash it down on* JONATHAN'S *unseen head when* HENNESSEY *runs in Down Right, shouts at* RENFIELD, *momentarily distracting his attention and his aim.* REN-FIELD *brings the stool down with a crash behind the sofa, but* JONATHAN *crawls out to Right just in time to escape it.* HENNESSEY *runs toward* RENFIELD *who darts Up Center.*)

HENNESSEY. Renfield! In God's name, what are you doing?

RENFIELD. I'm going to kill him. Then kill myself! You can't stop me. Nobody can stop me! (*As* JONA-THAN, *winded and gasping, tries to sit up on the floor,* HENNESSEY *vaults over the back of the sofa, surprising* RENFIELD *into leaping to one side. This gives* HEN-NESSEY *the advantage and he circles above* RENFIELD, *getting between him and the windows. In a half crouching position, arms crooked before him as though about to make a football tackle,* HENNESSEY *cautiously moves toward* RENFIELD *who begins backing away toward Left stairway.*) You've always been good to me, Hennessey. Now the kindest thing you can do is leave me alone. I will not die as Count Dracula would have me die. *Do you hear?* . . . I'll die as I choose. . . . The roof! The roof! I'll jump from the roof! (*He is up the Left stairs in two leaps and disappears into the hall-*

way. His insane laughter fades in the distance. HEN-
NESSEY *starts after him, then hesitates, looking back at
the dazed, panting* JONATHAN *who has dragged himself
to front of sofa, leaned against it, his head on the seat,
his exposed chest heaving as he sucks in air.* HENNES-
SEY *looks Left once more after* RENFIELD, *then at* JON-
ATHAN *and goes to him hastily.*)

HENNESSEY. Mr. Harker, are you all right? Did he
injure you?

JONATHAN. (*Between gasps.*) No—he just—surprised—the hell out of me! That little man—is stronger
—than he looks.

HENNESSEY. (*Helping him up onto the sofa.*) It's the
strength of the insane, sir. Sure you're all right?

JONATHAN. Yes. Run after him. Don't—let him—
hurt himself.

HENNESSEY. (*Starts Left on the run.*) Right! (*As*
HENNESSEY *races up Left stairway* DR. SEWARD *appears on the landing.*)

SEWARD. What is it? What's the trouble?

HENNESSEY. Come with me, Doctor. Renfield is on
his way to the roof. Wants to commit suicide.

SEWARD. He won't. Instead he'll run away. Let's go!
(HENNESSEY *runs out into Left hall followed by* DR.
SEWARD. JONATHAN *shakes his head to clear it, then
leans back against sofa, eyes closed. There is a silence,
broken only by* JONATHAN's *labored breathing. Then*
MINA *appears on the Left stairway landing. She is
wearing the brilliantly colored evening gown she carried earlier. She has lowered the neckline to a provocative level and the fact that the dress is skin tight, backless and designed for a voluptuary heightens the whole
startling change in her manner. Her descent of the
stairs is languid, seductive. Her expression is wanton.
She holds one hand behind her where, dangling from a
finger, we see the garland of Batswort and the crucifix
on its chain.* JONATHAN, *eyes closed, unaware of her
presence, is the object of her lascivious smile. She goes*

*to the bar where she drops garland and crucifix, her lips
curling with distaste. Then she goes above sofa, reaches
into breast pocket of* JONATHAN'S *jacket on sofa back,
takes his crucifix from pocket and, holding it at arm's
length, moves up and drops it into the fire. As FIRE
FLARES UP, as though by some hellish magic, she
gives* JONATHAN *a look of evil triumph. Then slowly
she approaches him till she stands behind the sofa just
above him. Her smile widens and we see her* fangs. *She
is bending down, her mouth nearing his throat when*
VAN HELSING *appears on Left landing and lets out a
warning shout:*)

VAN HELSING. Jonathan! For the love of God, look
out! (JONATHAN *looks up, sees* MINA *on the point of
biting his throat and leaps to his feet.*)

JONATHAN. My God! *Mina!* (MINA *swiftly moves
to fire bench and sits facing upstage.* VAN HELSING
crosses hastily to JONATHAN. *In the ensuing dialogue,
with* MINA'S *back to the audience plus being fairly well
covered by* JONATHAN *and* VAN HELSING *downstage
of her, she slips the trick fangs from her mouth and
conceals them in her bodice.* JONATHAN *stares at* VAN
HELSING, *then starts toward* MINA. VAN HELSING
catches him arm, pulls him away to Down Left.)

VAN HELSING. Jonathan, you must beware of her.
Had she bitten you, it would have been the start of your
becoming one of the Undead.

JONATHAN. I? Become a—?

VAN HELSING. At this advanced stage, even her kiss
carries that curse. I warn you, do not kiss Mina, no
matter how she pleads for it! (MINA *now rises, hurries
to desk, picks up the stake and wooden mallet and starts
toward balcony to throw them over the rail.* VAN HEL-
SING *sees this over* JONATHAN'S *shoulder.*) Jonathan,
stop her! (JONATHAN *turns, sees where* MINA *is
headed, races upstage and intercepts her at the window,
blocking her way.*)

JONATHAN. Mina, give me those. (*She laughs at him, puts them behind her back.*)

VAN HELSING. By force, Jonathan. Take them by force before she throws them over the railing!

JONATHAN. (*Advancing.*) Please, Mina? (*As she retreats* JONATHAN *makes a lunge, grabs her, pulls stake and mallet from her hands.*)

VAN HELSING. Give them to me. (*Getting them from* JONATHAN.) We'll guard these from now on.

MINA. (*Face twisted with fury.*) I hate you. I hate you both! You'll pay for this! . . . I know what you plan to do, but you'll never find him. Never, never! (*Laughing at them, she steps onto balcony and calls:*) They would kill you, do you hear? Murder you with their puny wooden stake and mallet!

VAN HELSING. (*Going up Left stairs.*) I'll lock these up. (*Halfway, he turns.*) I'd advise you to come with me.

JONATHAN (*Eyes fixed on* MINA.) In a minute.

VAN HELSING. Don't stay, Jonathan. It will break your heart. (VAN HELSING *exits above Left.* JONATHAN *reluctantly starts to follow, then looks once more at* MINA. *She assumes a pleasant smile, glides toward him enticingly.*)

MINA. (*With false innocence.*) Jonathan, dear, what made me say those wicked things? . . . It was just a game. I was teasing you. . . How wonderful that we are alone. We've had so little time together, my lover. Let us take advantage of this moment. (*She puts her arms around him, moving her hands shamelessly over his flesh beneath the tattered T-shirt.*) Kiss me, Jonathan. (*He begins to lean toward her. She is Circe, Jezebel, Messalina all in one.*) K-i-s-s me! (JONATHAN *weakens, slowly lowering his head to kiss her parted lips when* VAN HELSING *reappears on Left landing and runs down the steps, holding out a small phial of liquid.* MINA *sees the phial over* JONATHAN'S *shoulder, breaks from him with a cry, retreats to the fireplace*

*where she stands, face averted, her whole body trem-
bling, arms wide with her hands gripping the mantel
top.*)

JONATHAN. (*Turns bewildered.*) What—what is it?
What's that in your hand?

VAN HELSING. It is holy water, one more weapon
against Vampires. She cannot stand even the sight of it!
(*At fireplace* MINA *shudders at the words "holy water."*
VAN HELSING *takes* JONATHAN'S *arm, leads him up
Left stairs.*) Come, I need you. And you need me, to
guard you against yourself! (*They exit together Down
Left hallway.* MINA *looks over her shoulder after them,
her eyes seething with hatred.*)

MINA. That wizened little man! How I loathe him!
(*She sits on fire bench again, rocking back and forth,
her back to the audience.* RENFIELD *enters at the Right
side of open windows and backs into the room. He
peers Left but does not look behind him where* MINA
*sits. He closes windows quietly, then shuts curtains and
draperies, turns, sees her and gasps. She laughs softly.*)
How very amusing. We are both waiting for Count
Dracula.

RENFIELD. No! I don't want to be seen by anybody,
least of all by him. I'm running away. They're looking
for me everywhere, up and down fire escapes, through
the corridors, in the basement—but I've tricked them
again!

MINA. (*Rising.*) Forget them. They are unimpor-
tant. It is really he you're running from, isn't it? (*REN-
FIELD nods in mute terror.*) Poor fool, you'll never get
away from him.

RENFIELD. (*Edges Left away from her.*) Yes, I will.
I will. . . . Come with me. We'll escape together.

MINA. (*Laughs at him, stretches luxuriously.*) Why
should I run away? I look forward to the future—with
Dracula!

RENFIELD. And you call me fool. (*Backing Left toward stairs.*) Come, it's not too late. We can take the

elevator to the ground floor, run through the woods, somehow reach London, then go to the Far East where Dracula will never, never find us. (*By now* RENFIELD *has backed up onto the first step of Left stairway, unaware that behind him the BOOKCASE HAS SLOWLY SWUNG OPEN, away from the steps. Nor does he see the hand that appears from the edge of the bookcase reaching for him.*) You—you won't come? (MINA, *who sees both the opened bookcase and the reaching hand, shakes her head, watching fascinated.* DRACULA'S *hand now clamps over* RENFIELD'S *mouth, his other arm goes around* RENFIELD'S *throat, throttling him. BOOKCASE SWINGS OPEN WIDER and we see* DRACULA *completely.*)

DRACULA. Treacherous idiot! You thought to betray Dracula and *live?* (*He drags the panic-stricken, choking* RENFIELD *out of sight and the BOOKCASE SILENTLY SWINGS BACK INTO POSITION.* MINA *moves quickly to the bookcase, presses her ear to it, listening with sadistic joy.*)

RENFIELD. (*Offstage, strangling.*) Master, please—!

DRACULA. (*Offstage.*) Be still, you sniveling, craven little coward! How I have waited for this!

RENFIELD. (*First a scream, then weeping.*) Oh, Master, Master, for the love of God, do not kill me! . . . Mercy! Oh, have mercy! I am your slave for life and after death! . . . Please, please, Master! . . . No, no! Not that, not *that!* (*A peak of agonized screaming, then abrupt silence.* MINA, *whose whole body has been taut, now relaxes and her smile widens.*)

(VAN HELSING *runs in from Left, stake and mallet in hand, followed by* JONATHAN.)

VAN HELSING. What was that scream?

MINA. It was I.

VAN HELSING. That was no woman's scream. You're lying.

MINA. (*Moving away to Center.*) And if I am—?

JONATHAN. Mina, please tell us. What happened?

MINA. Let's make a bargain, shall we? I'll answer you if you'll tell me where you hope to destroy Count Dracula.

JONATHAN. No.

MINA. Too bad, my lover. It would be an experiment in thought transference. He can read my mind, you know, as I read his. Why not tell me? It would be interesting to prove that, without uttering a sound, I can warn him.

(DR. SEWARD *and* HENNESSEY *enter Down Right.*)

SEWARD. Renfield's done it again.

HENNESSEY. We covered the building, the basement, the roof—*everywhere!*

JONATHAN. Do you suppose he's gone back to Castle Carfax?

MINA. No, I don't think he'll go there any more.

SEWARD. Well, there's not a sign of him.

MINA. Oh, he can't be far. In fact, I believe you'll find a clue on the balcony. (*The men look at her puzzled, then* SEWARD *and* HENNESSEY *go Up Center followed by* JONATHAN *and* VAN HELSING. *Two of them open the draperies, the curtains, then pull the French windows open into the room and step back in horror.* RENFIELD'S *body lies across the balcony rail in a backbend, his bloody face upside down toward the audience.* DR. SEWARD, *the first to approach him, lifts* REN-FIELD'S *limp arm and feels for pulse.*)

VAN HELSING. (*Quietly.*) We are too late.

SEWARD. He's dead.

VAN HELSING. Poor lonely devil.

HENNESSEY. But, Doctor, who—?

JONATHAN. Count Dracula killed him, of course. Renfield said he would.

SEWARD. If only we had found him in time, locked him in his cell—

MINA. Where he was would not have mattered. He was destined to die. (*The four men look at her in momentary shock. Then* DR. SEWARD *takes charge:*)

SEWARD. Help me lift him off the rail. (*While* SEWARD, JONATHAN *and* HENNESSEY *get* RENFIELD'S *body down,* VAN HELSING *continues to look steadily at* MINA, *shaking his head.*)

MINA. Don't shake your fatuous head at me. I didn't kill him.

VAN HELSING. But you will kill, Mina, unless we save you. (*With a glance of contempt, she turns and walks away.* SEWARD *and* HENNESSEY *start carrying* RENFIELD *toward Down Right, one lifeless arm dangling at each step, his bloody head wobbling toward the audience.*)

SEWARD. I'll call the coroner.

VAN HELSING. (*Hurrying to* SEWARD.) No, have Hennessey do that. Arthur, you must come back immediately. It's urgent.

JONATHAN. (*Joins them Down Right.*) You mean because of the time?

VAN HELSING. Exactly. I've checked the Almanac. Daybreak is due in six minutes. If we are to trap him, it must be within—

JONATHAN. (*A monotone, to himself.*) Six minutes. (*During the four men's move to Down Right and their preoccupation with the corpse,* MINA *has followed at a distance, then mounted the Right stairway. She now stands on the landing unobserved and looking down on them all.*)

SEWARD. At times like this I have *duties,* Heinrich, but I'll hurry. (*He and* HENNESSEY *exit with* RENFIELD'S *body.* JONATHAN *and* VAN HELSING *hold Down Right, looking after them. In that quiet moment* MINA *regards them malevolently, then goes on upstairs out of sight. Neither* JONATHAN *nor* VAN HELSING *has seen her go.* VAN HELSING *crosses to desk, puts stake and*

mallet down, then feels through his pockets. JONATHAN
follows to Center.)

JONATHAN. (*Massaging back of his neck.*) Every
muscle, every nerve is tied up in a bowknot. Professor,
you don't seem tired at all.

VAN HELSING. Well, I'm the unofficial General for
our planned attack. Generals are always alert before
battle. (*Digging in pockets again.*) Except I'm not too
alert. I seem to have lost my pipe. I'm getting as addle-
brained as Sybil.

JONATHAN. Where's Mina?

VAN HELSING. (*Glances about.*) I don't know. Perhaps out on the balcony. (JONATHAN *goes to windows,
looks off both Left and Right.* VAN HELSING *gives up
his pocket search, takes cigarette from desk box.*) Well,
I guess there's nothing for it.

JONATHAN. She's not out here. Professor, come take
a look.

VAN HELSING. (*Lighting cigarette as he joins* JONA-
THAN *at windows.*) For Mina?

JONATHAN. No, over there. There's a faint light coming up on the horizon.

VAN HELSING. (*Looks off, then studies watch.*) Five
minutes and fourteen seconds. He *must* come. He's ar-
rogant enough to welcome the challenge. . . . You
have your crucifix?

JONATHAN. (*Points to jacket on sofa back.*) There,
safe in my pocket—but I think I'll get reinforcements.
(*Starts for Left stairs.*)

VAN HELSING. Where are you going?

JONATHAN. Professor, it's not that I don't have faith.
I believe in the divine good the crucifix represents, but
I want material aid. There's an old sword hanging in
the music room. (*Sprinting up Left stairway.*) If I'm
to meet Count Dracula in combat, I'd like to be armed!

VAN HELSING. Don't be too long, or too far away to
hear me call if—

JONATHAN. It's down the hall, but I'll hear you. (*As*

he exits into Left hall he almost bowls over SYBIL *on her way in, Dickens in hand. She backs onto stair landing, looking after him.*)

SYBIL. Great heavens! When I left here he was walking in his sleep! Where did he get all that energy?

VAN HELSING. Heredity, I assume. (*He wanders to fireplace, flicks cigarette ash into coals.*)

SYBIL. Thank goodness things have quieted down. I was dozing over Dickens and the screams kept waking me up. (VAN HELSING, *again studying his watch, does not answer. Seeing he has his back to her,* SYBIL *sidles up to the bar, produces the now empty sherry decanter from the folds of her robe and sets it down. She gives a small, ladylike hiccup which makes* VAN HELSING *turn.*) Radishes. They always upset me. (*She moves quickly but with care to Right stairs and starts up.*) Forgive my deserting you, but I think I'll take "Dombey and Son" to bed. (*She waves the book at him, has a further digestive disturbance, and exits upstairs Right.*)

VAN HELSING. (*Looks at the empty room, then again at his watch.*) Dawn in five minutes. (*To desk, picks up stake, slaps it against his palm.*) If it is to be, it must be within those five little eons. (*MUSIC BEGINS SOFTLY, The Dracula Leitmotif, and once more FOG DRIFTS IN the open windows.* VAN HELSING *sees it, puts stake down and crosses to fireplace where he stands watching, waiting.*) It is to be. And now. *Now!* (*MUSIC HOLDS UNDER as, with no sound of wind, the WINDOW CURTAINS MOVE SLIGHTLY, then fall still. A DIM FOLLOW SPOT IRISES IN at windows' center.* PRODUCTION NOTE: *This is not the standard circular follow spot but a slim, vertical strip of light focused to represent a man's height and width. SPOTLIGHT MOVES from window toward desk and DESK CHAIR MOVES BACK from desk unaided. Then CHAIR MOVES IN TO DESK again as though the invisible* DRACULA *had sat down.*) Ah, I have a visitor. A distinguished guest—even when invisible. (*A *slight bow.*) Good morning, Count Dracula. (*He starts toward desk. Immediately CHAIR MOVES BACK AWAY FROM DESK.*) Leaving? So soon? What a pity. Can't I prevail upon you to—? (*He stops as SPOTLIGHT MOVES toward sofa, DIPS DOWN SLIGHTLY for the invisible* DRACULA'S *"sitting" and SOFA'S CENTER SEAT CUSHION SINKS IN THE MIDDLE as though sat upon.*) That's better. Stay awhile. Of course, it is late in the morning for you to pay a social call. Nearly daybreak. But, don't go! I have something rather unusual to show you. (VAN HELSING *goes up to the bar. As he does the SPOTLIGHT "RISES" from sofa and the SEAT CUSHION SPRINGS BACK TO FULL PLUMPNESS. SPOTLIGHT MOVES to Right staircase and "mounts" steps.* VAN HELSING *comes down to sofa carrying a sprig of dry weed with withered flower.*) It's a plant I don't think you've often encountered. It's called The Devil's-Paint-Brush, or Hawkweed, and it— (*He notices cushion is no longer indented, that spotlight has moved to stair landing.*) Oh, *there* you are! For a moment I thought you'd— (*Crossing to stairs.*) I don't believe she's up there. In fact, Wilhelmina seems to have vanished. But then, as a gifted clairvoyant, doubtless you know of her whereabouts. (*FOLLOW SPOT IRISES OUT on stair landing as though* DRACULA *had climbed on up out of sight. MUSIC FADES OUT.* VAN HELSING *goes up one step and stops. All the poise, all the aplomb he mustered for the invisible* DRACULA *are gone. He begins to talk nervously to himself:*) But if she *is* up there, unprotected— (*Runs toward bell cord, finds it's gone.*) Hell! Where's the bell cord? . . . The buzzer. The desk buzzer! (*Hurries to desk, then stops in distress.*) Oh, Lord! What's the combination to get Wesley? (*Mumbles rapidly:*) Three-longs-and-one-short, or three-shorts-and-a-long? (*With mounting desperation.*) I'll try both! (*Pushes buzzer repeatedly, then runs up Left stairs and calls:*) Jonathan! Jonathan, come quickly! (*Waits. No answer.*) Jonathan, where are you? (*He gives up, runs to desk, examines stake and mallet nervously, looks toward Right stairs.*) This is the moment. He's here—and I'm alone. God help me, what am I to do?

(WESLEY *enters sleepily from Down Right in pajamas and slippers, fighting his way into a bathrobe and losing the battle with the cord.*)

WESLEY. I think somebody buzzed me, but the signal was all mixed up.

VAN HELSING. For the love of God, never mind! Find Dr. Seward. Tell him to come here fast!

WESLEY. (*Through a yawn.*) Where is he, sir?

VAN HELSING. (*Wildly, pointing Down Right.*) *In there* somewhere! Find him! *FIND HIM!*

WESLEY. (*Catches the urgency, stops in the middle of a stretch.*) Yes, sir! (*As* WESLEY *dashes out Down Right* VAN HELSING *races to Left steps again, calls up:*)

VAN HELSING. Jonathan! (*He waits a few moments, then goes back to desk worried, apprehensive, leans on desk with both fists clenched, head down and his back to Right stairway.* DRACULA *appears soundlessly on the Right stair landing. He comes down the steps with slow enjoyment, his glittering eyes fixed on* VAN HELSING's *back.*) All our carefully laid plans—ruined. I'm alone, only one third of the triumvirate, and I shall fail. (*Raises his head, looks into mirror on desk.*) I look like a failure. (*Behind him* DRACULA *takes a heavy brass candlestick from the mantel, lays candle noiselessly on mantel top, then raises candlestick as a bludgeon and moves with panther-like stealth toward his prey.* VAN HELSING *appears to be looking into mirror, studying his own face, but actually his body is angled so that he sees* DRACULA's *approach from the corner of his eye. At the moment* DRACULA *is ready to strike,*

VAN HELSING *steps calmly aside.*) Clever. You counted on my not seeing you, since no mirror reflects the Vampire. I saw you peripherally.

DRACULA. Damn you! Damn your knowledge and your mirror! (*He hurls the candlestick and smashes the mirror to bits.*) I need no weapon. I'll kill you with my bare hands! (*He starts toward* VAN HELSING *who produces the phial of holy water from inner pocket and holds it up.* DRACULA *recoils with a cry of fury.* VAN HELSING *backs up to French windows, keeping his eyes warily on* DRACULA. *Still holding phial before him with one hand, he reaches back with the other, closes first one window, then the second.* DRACULA, *who has watched with bitter amusement, now gives a long, mocking laugh.*) Pathetic fool! There are other ways out. For example, that door. (*He starts toward door Down Right only to have it open and* SEWARD *enter.* SEWARD *stops with a gasp as he sees* DRACULA *who turns to* VAN HELSING.) A more interesting door now—for it frames an elderly lamb, waiting for slaughter! (*Slowly raising his hands to throttle* SEWARD, *he approaches him with pleasurable deliberation.*)

VAN HELSING. Arthur! Your crucifix! (DRACULA *stops, watches maliciously as* SEWARD *searches in breast pocket, then all pockets for his crucifix.*)

SEWARD. It's gone! (DRACULA'S *laugh is demonic as again he starts slowly toward* SEWARD, *hands outstretched.* VAN HELSING'S *eye falls on the weighted Batswort garland* MINA *left on the bar. Behind* DRACULA'S *back, he runs to bar, grabs up the garland, hurries Center and hurls it over* DRACULA'S *head to* SEWARD.)

VAN HELSING. Use this! The Batswort! (SEWARD *catches the weighted flowers, holds them up at eye level toward* DRACULA.)

DRACULA. Devil damn you! (*Turns away to Center, shielding his eyes from the blossoms, then glances Left.*) But there is still this staircase, gentlemen! (*He runs toward Left stairs as* JONATHAN *appears on Left landing, 19th Century dress sword in hand. With sword before him, he starts down the steps.* DRACULA *holds his ground.*) Ah, Sir Lancelot with shining sword! Steel cannot kill me, Mr. Harker, nor your bullets—as you discovered earlier this morning.

JONATHAN. Damn you! *Damn* you! I'll see you in hell!

DRACULA. Very likely—but you'll go there first! (*Makes a sudden lunge at* JONATHAN, *who, thrown off guard, backs up a step.*)

SEWARD. (*Shouting.*) Your cross, Jonathan!

VAN HELSING. Hold your crucifix before him!

(DRACULA *stops on steps below* JONATHAN, *waiting, watching with amusement.* JONATHAN, *passing sword from hand to hand, feverishly feels the outside of all trouser pockets.* DRACULA *turns, glides to sofa, picks up Jonathan's jacket and tosses it to him.*)

DRACULA. Here, Mr. Harker. *Look* for it! (VAN HELSING *and* SEWARD *watch anxiously,* DRACULA *looks on with a sardonic smile as* JONATHAN *fingers jacket breast pocket, all other pockets, then looks up bewildered.*)

JONATHAN. It's—

DRACULA. Gone? You surprise me. (*With a triumphant laugh,* DRACULA *starts again toward* JONATHAN, *now with measured tread, eyeing him with a hypnotic stare, his hands before him in traditional mesmeric position.* JONATHAN *lets the sword sag. The jacket drops to the steps. Slowly he begins to retreat, backing up toward the landing, his eyelids growing heavy, his head beginning to nod.*)

VAN HELSING. (*Shouts in alarm.*) Jonathan! Use your will power!

SEWARD. In God's name, don't let him hypnotize you! (JONATHAN, *backed all the way up to the landing, now opens his eyes, shakes his head to clear it. Suddenly he grasps the sword high up on the blade, turns it lengthwise point down, and holds it before* DRACULA, *its handle and blade resembling a cross.*)

DRACULA. (*A hoarse whisper of fury.*) The handle of your sword—!

JONATHAN. Yes! (*Thrusts it to* DRACULA'S *face.*) It forms a cross! (*With a frightful cry, savage and atavistic,* DRACULA *turns, runs down the steps followed by* JONATHAN. DRACULA *starts toward windows where he veers from the sight of Van Helsing's phial of sacred water. He races Right only to have* SEWARD *hold the Batswort garland aloft again. Livid, snarling, trapped,* DRACULA *backs away from them all to behind sofa, looking from one to the other.*)

VAN HELSING. (*To* SEWARD, *coming downstage.*) Thank God you came! I was afraid Wesley wouldn't find— (*Turns.*) And you, Jonathan! I despaired, thinking you hadn't heard me. (*A quick glance at this watch and his tone becomes triumphant.*) In three minutes the sun will rise. He will be powerless. We shall rid the earth of Dracula forever!

DRACULA. (*Breaks into a long, derisive laugh.*) I laugh at you, gentlemen. . . . You, Mr. Harker, with your makeshift crucifix. You, Professor, with your godly water. And you, Doctor, with your blossoms of Batswort. These devices serve only to keep me at bay, to keep me from killing each of you now—but my revenge will come. I spread it over centuries—and time is on my side. I will wait. . . . I have made an art of waiting—with many hundreds of years' practice. (*Turns sharply to* VAN HELSING.) *Yes,* Professor Van Helsing, you have read of the Fifteenth Century Count Voivode Dracula. Now *look* upon him! I am he! (*Taking in all three.*) Already my life span outnumbers your combined three lives by centuries. *Many* centuries, gentlemen. Long after you are forgotten dust, I shall still walk the earth and rule the night! . . . And you think to kill me, the man Death himself cannot overtake? You think to hold Count Dracula captive for three minutes till sun-up? You will not hold him three seconds!

VAN HELSING. Close in on him. With the first ray of sunlight, we seize him! (*They move in.* VAN HELSING *comes downstage,* SEWARD *to Right end of sofa,* JONATHAN *to Left end.* DRACULA, *behind sofa, half turns so that his back is to the audience, twisting his head to watch each of his captors.*)

(MINA *enters on Right stairway landing.*)

MINA. Dracula, I will help you. They will not stop me nor harm me. (*Looks at the three men with contempt as she descends.*) Their sentimental human hearts will not let them.

DRACULA. Don't interfere. These incompetent milksops can keep me here no more than they can keep us apart. You will come to me—now!

MINA. Where? Where shall I come?

DRACULA. Make your mind receptive to my thoughts. My mind will reach out to yours. I shall *will* you to come where I lie by day. There you will wait for the dark—when I shall rise again. Then, for all time, you shall be my bride!

(*Gradually the sky cyclorama has been growing light. Now soft MORNING LIGHT is seen through the windows.*)

VAN HELSING. Day is breaking! Seize him. Hold him fast! I'll block the windows!

(DRACULA, *still with back to audience, now pulls the hood of cape over his head.* JONATHAN *and* SEWARD *grab him by each shoulder. As they struggle the three of them move toward the secret panel in*

Right wall. [PRODUCTION NOTE: *Dracula's cape with hood is not the same cape worn in Acts One and Two. It is a special cape, floor length, made with a light wire frame to hold the shape of Dracula's shoulders, its hood wired to retain the outline of the back of his head once he's out of the cape.*] *Once the three men are in position in front of the secret panel,* MINA *screams, runs Up Center to* VAN HELSING *and fights him in her effort to open the windows. During* MINA'S *scream and her run across the stage—which should distract audience attention—*DRACULA *ducks down behind the cape with* SEWARD *and* JONATHAN *still holding cape's framework, making it appear* DRACULA *is still in it.* DRACULA *now "escapes" through the low, narrow secret panel, concealed by the position and width of the cape. The moment he has got away and the panel has closed,* SEWARD *and* JONATHAN *continue their struggle with the cape for a few seconds, working their way* downstage away from the panel. *Then, in apparent amazement, they stop, let the cape sag, shake it in bewilderment, come Center examining it, then throw it to the floor.*)

JONATHAN. He's gone! (*Points to sofa.*) No, he's back there! (*He and* SEWARD *whirl sofa endwise toward audience, search all around it.*)

SEWARD. It's impossible—but he got away!

VAN HELSING. How could he? The windows were shut. (*He goes up to windows, tests them.* JONATHAN *and* SEWARD *follow him.*) They're still shut! He used neither staircase. (*While they are involved at the windows,* MINA *has crossed to Left stairs and stopped by the pivot bookcase, out of the men's eyesight. She stares front, eyes vacant.*)

MINA. (*Tonelessly.*) I hear. . . . Yes, Dracula, the hidden vault in Castle Carfax. . . The crypt through the secret passage. . . . Yes, yes. . . . Now I know the way. I am coming. (*Behind her the BOOKCASE SLOWLY SWINGS OPEN. She turns, steps through the opening and disappears in the blackness. BOOKCASE SILENTLY CLOSES behind her.* VAN HELSING *leaves window, comes down to desk, picks up stake and mallet, then drops them hopelessly.*)

JONATHAN. He's on the balcony. He's got to be! Where else—? (*Opens French windows fast.*)

SEWARD. Don't be foolish, Jonathan. How would he get there? Professor Van Helsing stood right here in front of the windows. You saw him! They were never opened.

JONATHAN. Just the same, I'm looking. (*He runs onto balcony and out of sight to the Right.*)

SEWARD. (*Goes to* VAN HELSING, *puts arm about his shoulder.*) Don't despair, Heinrich. We'll get him. Perhaps tomorrow—

VAN HELSING. No. You see how far advanced Mina is toward being his creature? Tomorrow will be too late.

SEWARD. Oh, no. I pray that—

VAN HELSING. We have all prayed. It seems our prayers were not heard.

JONATHAN. (*Shouting, offstage on balcony.*) Professor! Dr. Seward!

SEWARD. (*Hurries to windows.*) What is it?

VAN HELSING. (*Follows.*) Jonathan, what's the matter?

JONATHAN. (*Runs in from balcony.*) It's Mina! Mina!

SEWARD. What about her?

VAN HELSING. Where is she?

JONATHAN. She's in my car, that's where! (*Points off angrily.*) Mina's down there, driving away in my car!

SEWARD. She's going after him.

VAN HELSING. (*As they look at one another with*

sudden realization.) She'll *lead us to him.* To his coffin—in Castle Carfax!

JONATHAN. God, *YES!* Quick!

VAN HELSING. (*Grabs up stake and mallet.*) Arthur, hurry! We'll follow in your car!

SEWARD. Mina is a fast driver.

JONATHAN. I'm *faster!* Come on! (*He snatches his jacket from bottom of Left stairway, is flinging it on over torn T-shirt and bounding up the steps, followed by* VAN HELSING *and* SEWARD *as ALL LIGHTS IN FAST DIM OUT.*)

CURTAIN

(*HOUSE LIGHTS REMAIN OUT. MUSIC UP as "fill" for fast set change.*)

ACT THREE

SCENE 2

SCENE: *The Crypt at daybreak.*

PRODUCTION NOTE: *This brief scene can be played in small inset within the play's main setting. The same stairway Left, disguised with stone balustrade downstage, can be used unrecognized in the dim lighting.*

SETTING: *Dracula's open coffin IN A POOL OF LIGHT is well downstage at a slight angle, almost parallel to the proscenium arch. The coffin is without lid. Its upper half of its downstage side is hinged to hang open later. Aside from the coffin, little else is visible except cobwebs and ancient masonry which looks as though it would crumble at the touch. The stone stairway Left, leading down into the crypt, is not lighted. Light "spill" from Center stage should suffice.*

At Rise: Dracula, *without cape, lies in the coffin, his head to stage Right. MUSIC, which played through scene change, now BECOMES SOMBER, FUNEREAL and HOLDS UNDER through* Mina's *entrance, then GRADUALLY DIES AWAY. As LIGHTS FADE IN,* Mina *enters down Left steps, barely seen in the light spill. She descends slowly, looking back over her shoulder. At the bottom step she waits, listens a moment, then smiles contentedly.*

Mina. They will not find me. Let them search the day through. They will never find me here— (*Goes to coffin.*) nor you, my love. You are safe! (*Moves upstage of coffin, looks down tenderly.*) How beautiful you are. Pallid, cold—sleeping in your living death. (*Touches his face.*) Your cheeks are icy to my fingers. (*Goes down on one knee so that her face is level with his.*) How thrilling to touch that cold, cold cheek! . . . Soon, Dracula, I shall sleep through the daylight hours with you and then, by dark, we shall roam the earth together—seeking blood.

(*The voices of* Jonathan, Seward *and* Van Helsing *in mumbled ad lib are heard in the distance.* Mina's *eyes narrow, she rises quickly, steps Left and listens.*)

Jonathan. (*Off, now audible.*) This way! Look, there's her trail!
Mina. What trail? I left no trail.
Van Helsing. (*Off.*) Watch yourself! These walls have jagged stones.
Mina. Damn them! (*Runs to above coffin.*) Dracula, I swear, I left no trail.

JONATHAN. (*Off.*) How did Mina get here alive? She raced that car like a bat from hell.

MINA. A bat! (*Kneels again above coffin, speaking rapidly, fervently:*) Dracula, my love, if only you had killed me, made me wholly a Vampire. Why did you wait? . . . Then I could have entered here as you do—soaring through the dawn, leaving no trail. (*Beating her fist on coffin edge.*) I think I'm going mad. What possible clue could I have left to guide them to this secret place?

JONATHAN. (*Off, even nearer.*) I see light ahead. Come on!

SEWARD. (*Off.*) Careful, Jonathan! There are deep pits down here.

MINA. I wish the pit of hell itself would engulf you! (*She sinks out of sight behind coffin where, unseen by audience, she slips* fangs *hidden in her bodice into her mouth.*)

(JONATHAN *enters down the stairs, his flashlight aimed more at steps, floor and audience than in coffin's direction. Behind him comes* SEWARD *with flashlight.* VAN HELSING *follows carrying stake and mallet.*)

JONATHAN. Watch those steps. They crumble underfoot. (*Turns and flashlight shines on coffin.*) *There!* There he is!

VAN HELSING. We've found him!

JONATHAN. (*At downstage side of coffin, beams flashlight directly on* DRACULA'S *head.*) God, how I hate that face! (*Loosens clasp, lowers hinged side panel of coffin, revealing* DRACULA *from waist up.*) Look at him! (SEWARD *and* VAN HELSING *join him. All three peer silently into coffin.*)

SEWARD. But where is Mina?

JONATHAN. (*Looks up.*) She's not here?

VAN HELSING. She *has* to be! (*They separate, play-*

ing their flashlights into dark corners, searching. MINA'S
*hands come up like claws from behind the coffin, then
she rises, looks upon them with consummate hate. As*
JONATHAN *turns and sees her, she moves toward him
like a tigress,* fangs bared. VAN HELSING *grabs* JONA-
THAN'S *arm, pulls him back.* MINA *stops at coffin's Left
end.*) Wait, Jonathan. Don't go near her.

JONATHAN. But I—

VAN HELSING. Listen to me! (*He leads* JONATHAN
well downstage Left, motioning SEWARD *to join them.
As men move downstage,* MINA *goes to below coffin,
her back to them. She bends far over, as though kissing*
DRACULA *and, with the action thus covered, removes
fangs, tucks them into bodice.*) She will fight us, try to
stop us.

MINA. (*Caressing* DRACULA'S *face.*) I will not let
them kill you, my love.

VAN HELSING. (*Leads men even farther downstage.*)
We must trick her, plan each move like a chess game.
(*He whispers and they lean in to hear.*)

MINA. (*Laughs contemptuously.*) Let them plot and
scheme. They will never succeed, babbling little fools!
(*The three men separate.* JONATHAN *arcs well below*
MINA *to far Right and upstage. As* MINA *starts upstage for him,* VAN HELSING *quickly moves to above
coffin,* SEWARD *to its Left end.* MINA *turns, starts for
them and* JONATHAN *grabs her from behind, pinions
her arms, pulls her far upstage Right. She struggles violently, heaping threats and imprecations ad lib upon*
JONATHAN *while* SEWARD *joins* VAN HELSING *above
coffin, takes stake from him, places it carefully over*
DRACULA'S *heart—in actuality, between his chest and
left arm—and* VAN HELSING *lifts the mallet high and
holds it still.* MINA, *trapped, helpless, watches with horror as* VAN HELSING *delivers the first of three heavy,
deliberate blows on head of stake, held in place by*
SEWARD. *With each blow,* MINA *cries out and* DRACULA
writhes in the coffin. At each strike there are WEIRD

*SOUND EFFECTS ECHOING AND DYING while
PSYCHEDELIC LIGHTS PLAY BRIEFLY OVER
AUDIENCE. SOUND LEVEL AND LIGHT IN-
TENSITY INCREASE to climactic height for third,
final blow. On that last strike of the mallet,* DRACULA
*lets out a horrifying scream, his arms shoot up, his
hands reaching for* VAN HELSING *and* SEWARD, *then
fall limply over the sides of the coffin. PSYCHE-
DELIC LIGHTS AND WEIRD SOUND EFFECTS
DIE AWAY. When it is all over, there is a prolonged
wail of anguish from* MINA *and she faints into* JONA-
THAN'S *arms. Silently,* VAN HELSING *and* SEWARD *lift*
DRACULA'S *arms, put them back within the coffin and
close the hinged, downstage side panel.*)

VAN HELSING. It is done.

SEWARD. He is truly dead?

VAN HELSING. For eternity. (*Moves to below coffin.*) I have committed murder, yet I feel no guilt.

SEWARD. (*Follows him.*) Nor I, Heinrich.

JONATHAN. (*Carries* MINA *down to them.*) Help me
bring her to, Doctor. Rub her wrists.

SEWARD. (*Rubbing* MINA'S *left wrist.*) Take her
other wrist, Heinrich. Get her circulation going. (VAN
HELSING *nods, briskly rubs her right wrist.*)

JONATHAN. When she comes to, will she—be Mina
again?

VAN HELSING. (*Hesitates.*) We can only hope, Jonathan.

SEWARD. There, she's coming round. Set her on her
feet. (*As* JONATHAN, *still supporting her, sets* MINA *in
standing position, she opens her eyes and looks at the
three faces round her.*)

MINA. I—I fainted, didn't I?

JONATHAN. Yes, darling, right into my arms.

MINA. Oh, Jonathan! (*Steadies herself, looks around
the vault uncertainly.*) Why—why are we in this dark,
cold place?

JONATHAN. Well, you were here first, and we came—

MINA. (*Gaining composure.*) I was here first? (*Slowly.*) Yes—yes, I remember. How did you find me?

JONATHAN. Your footprints in the dust, darling. They guided us like arrows on a map!

MINA. (*Sees coffin, goes to it, stops with a gasp.*) Count Dracula! I remember now. I tried to prevent you from— He's dead, isn't he? You killed him.

VAN HELSING. Yes, Wilhelmina.

SEWARD. To save you.

MINA. How kind and loving you are—and what a frightful experience it has been for each of you.

JONATHAN. Put it all out of your mind, love. (*Hugging her.*) Just think of it as a nightmare.

MINA. A nightmare. Oh, *yes*, Jonathan! (*Kisses him.*) But what a heavenly way to wake up! (*They meld in an embrace and a lingering kiss as—*)

(*THE LIGHTS FADE.*)

CURTAIN

MAGIC TRICKS
and
SPECIAL EFFECTS
(In sequence as used in performance)

Note: For small sleight-of-hand apparatus Count Dracula needs for magic tricks in the play (such as Cigarette Vanisher, Flash Paper, etc.), if there is no magic supply house in your city, write to The Society of American Magicians, 20 Sutton Place South, New York, N.Y. 10022. Enclose self-addressed-stamped envelope and request name and address of magic supply firm nearest you.

ACT ONE

CIGARETTE WITH FLAMING TIP PRODUCED FROM THIN AIR

When Count Dracula produces a lighted cigarette from nowhere, the tip is literally flaming, not merely lighted. The flame is to catch every eye in the audience instantly.

Materials needed: A standard size cigarette (not King size), wooden kitchen safety match, Flash Paper from magic shop, sharp knife or safety razor blade, small tweezers, scissors, beige or flesh colored masking tape or Scotch Magic Transparent Tape, and two small strips of abrasive striking paper from kitchen match box.

Construction: Loosen tobacco by rolling cigarette gently between fingers. With tweezers remove about ½ inch of tobacco from flame end, taking care not to tear cigarette paper. Sharpen wooden end of kitchen match, making a point at least ½ inch long. If match stick is square or thick, whittle it smooth and round the full length of stem.

Flash Paper usually is packaged in 3 to 4 inch squares. Cut a 1½ inch square (through size may vary according to desired effect) and fold it twice to form a ¾ inch square of four thicknesses. Make a small hole in center of folded square with an awl or tip of one scissor blade. Insert sharp point of whittled match into hole and push Flash Paper up just *under* match head. Crush or wad paper upward toward match head but *do not let it cover head.*

118

Insert point of match into hollowed out end of cigarette. Carefully force match all the way down until wad of Flash Paper is inside and *below* top of cigarette paper. Match head must remain slightly *above* Flash Paper and *above* end of cigarette.

Cut two 2 inch strips of "striking paper" from kitchen match box. Glue these strips side by side onto a piece of pliable cardboard, forming a small oblong to fit into palm. With beige or flesh colored masking tape or Scotch tape, adhere oblong abrasive paper to palm of left hand.

Performance: When Jonathan offers Count Dracula a cigarette, he replies, "I have my own," and turns away. As other characters hold audience attention, Count Dracula unobtrusively takes prepared trick cigarette from low inner pocket of tail coat and "palms" it, concealed from audience in semirelaxed right hand. His left hand, with abrasive paper attached, he holds at about waist height, open palm up. With right thumb and two fingers he holds cigarette about one inch below head of match, then quickly brings cigarette (match head) down across abrasive paper in left palm and continues the circular motion of his right hand by moving it sidewise to his right and then high over his head. At the same time, it is important to *put thumb under base of cigarette* and *slide cigarette up* between the first two fingers of right hand, getting it into smoking position and getting finger tips away from the flame. He must not look up until cigarette is above head. If the whole movement of striking and raising cigarette high is done rapidly, the Flash Paper will not ignite till cigarette is elevated. *Then* Count Dracula looks up, making a gesture as though pulling cigarette out of flaming air. He blows out the flame casually, puts cigarette to his lips and begins to smoke. Since the match creates a sharp sulphuric taste, it is wise not to inhale the first puffs. The burned match head will be evident to those onstage but not to the audience.

Count Dracula leaves the stage within a minute after this trick, removes abrasive paper from his palm, leaving it on prop table for Act Two when the trick is repeated with a variation.

During early rehearsals the actor can work with just an ordinary cigarette with kitchen match inserted alone, omitting Flash Paper until later. Thus he can perfect the striking, the timing of the unbroken circular move of the right hand, the lifting of cigarette over his head and, most important, learn that—if properly executed—he will not get his fingers burned!

DRAPERIES AND GAUZE CURTAINS
OPEN UNAIDED

The two sets of curtains are on separate traveler tracks and controlled by drawstrings from *backstage Left* of French windows. Small hole in scenery, through which drawstrings move over backstage pulleys, is concealed by top Left outer fold of draperies.

Two pairs of "dummy" drawstrings, one for each set of curtains, are behind Left edge of Left drapery. These dummy lines, which will move in an unbroken journey-to-nowhere from *onstage* pulleys at window's top to pulleys on the set's baseboard, are out of sight until a performer moves the drapery aside, lets the audience see him grasp the cords, then allows drapery to fall back into position, covering his hands and cords simultaneously. Thus his action with dummy lines seems to synchronize with the actual drawstring operation from backstage.

It is safest to have all real manipulation of curtains come from behind the scenes. It is, of course, essential when curtains open unaided, as though by "magic".

FRENCH WINDOWS BLOWN OPEN BY "WIND"
FOR ENTRANCE OF BAT

This effect is achieved via strong, thin, *lusterless* wires attached to *lower front base* of each window, near point where windows meet when closed. Wires are threaded through large screw eyes in stage floor (one near bar in Up Left corner, one near Left corner of fireplace) and pulled simultaneously from offstage when blast of wind supposedly forces windows to open into the room. Wires may be detached after Act One since this effect is not repeated.

If fine piano wire is used, long a mainstay in stage illusions, staining it with iodine renders it practically invisible from a short distance.

FOG ROLLS IN THROUGH OPEN WINDOWS

Fog making machine may be rented or purchased from any large theatrical supply house. Since ammonia is one of the chemicals used to create stage fog, its vapor is pungent if used to excess. The stage should be cleared of fog with electric fans or other means once curtain is down on Act One.

Fog is used again in Act Three, Scene 1, but *very briefly so* that little ammonic vapor accumulates or drifts toward front row spectators. Occasionally the chugging of fog machine motor is audible and may have to be covered by music.

BAT FLIES IN THROUGH WINDOW, DISAPPEARS ABOVE RIGHT COLUMN

Three prop bats exactly alike are needed for the play's production; one for Act One, and two for separate flights in Act Two. Bats' frameworks are constructed of malleable wire, such as chicken wire, and covered with dull black cloth. Bats should be larger than life-size with bodies 18" long and wing spans of 24".

Bat for Act One is pre-set backstage *above* and *well beyond* French windows and held in place by "trip line." 100 pound test black fishing line, also fastened above and beyond windows, runs through fine black wire loop attached to top of bat's body, and is tied off at other end *behind* top of Right column. This fishing line serves as a "track" for bat's flight.

When trip line is released on cue to free bat, a *second* black fishing line, fastened to front of bat's body, is rapidly reeled in by crew member on tall A-ladder off Right, making bat fly in through window, over Mina on sofa and up out of sight behind Right column. To effect proper swiftness of bat's flight a very fast, very large fishing rod reel is needed, the type used for deep sea fishing.

FLASH POT

These may be bought or rented from theatrical supply firms. It is best to sink flash pot (which is about 4" wide by 8" long) into hearth floor behind brass foot rail where it is completely hidden from audience. This same flash pot is used again in Act Two, reloaded during intermission.

The flash on cue is controlled electrically from backstage. Experiment, prior to technical rehearsals, to ascertain the right amount of flash powder needed. *Do not Overload.* If flash pot is used with common sense and caution there should be no fire hazzard. Even with the correct amount of powder for the desired effect, it is well to have fireplace front made of metal sheeting and painted to simulate wood, stone or whatever. And, axiomatic for all stage productions, window draperies and gauze curtains must be fire-proofed even though those Left of fireplace are a few feet away.

It is advisable to have an "understudy" flash pot, also sunk into hearth floor and concealed behind foot rail, in case the regular flash pot fails to perform.

"JUMPING OFF" PLATFORM AND RAMP

See set diagram. Ramp offstage Right and a running start give Count Dracula momentum for a flying leap into the room. If lack of space precludes a ramp backstage, he simply jumps into the room from platform. His sudden appearance is still effective, though not as fast and thereby a bit less startling.

Since the opening in the set beyond Right column is narrow, the performer must gather the fullness of his cape behind him with one hand to prevent its catching on scenery. Once he has cleared the opening, he releases his hold and the cape billows out as he lands upstage of sofa.

VAMPIRE FANGS

Two sets of fangs are needed, one for Dracula and one for Mina. White plastic fangs are available at most Joke and Novelty shops. Or your Technical Director can construct two sets, using trimmed, pointed white plastic stays (from men's shirt collars) for the fangs, then attaching them to a band to hold them in place when band is slipped under actor's upper lip.

Since it is difficult for performers to speak clearly with fangs in place neither Count Dracula nor Mina has any dialogue whenever fangs are used.

For the best false fangs, but most expensive, your local dentist can make them to fit over the natural teeth of actors playing the two Vampire roles.

ACT TWO

GAUZE CURTAINS BLOWING IN THE WIND

You will need to experiment with two silent-motored electric fans as to their proper placement at offstage ends of the set's balcony platform. Fans on the actual balcony floor may prove a traffic block for cast and crew backstage. Electric fans on high stands or fans hung from above and aimed down toward window curtains will serve best.

Dependent upon the distance between fans and curtains, you may find household electric fans not powerful enough and will need to resort to stronger, larger exhaust fans such as those used to ventilate attics or large offices.

MINA'S SCARF PRODUCED FROM THE AIR
BY COUNT DRACULA

The effect is that Mina's chiffon scarf from Act One springs magically from Count Dracula's finger tips. This is done with standard magician's apparatus called "The Silk Appearer," nominally priced and obtainable at any magic shop. Full written directions accompany each purchase.

BURNING CIGARETTE EXTINGUISHED
IN DRACULA'S PALM

After Count Dracula has made his second flaming cigarette appear, he apparently extinguishes it in his lightly closed palm. When he opens his palm, the cigarette has vanished.

The trick is accomplished with the aid of magician's small apparatus aptly called "The Cigarette Vanisher." It is inexpensive, simple to operate and available with full directions in any magic shop or magician's supply firm.

BAT FLIES FROM TOP OF RIGHT COLUMN
AND OUT FRENCH WINDOWS

This second prop bat's flight is exactly the reverse of bat flight in Act One. Bat is pre-set behind top of Right column, held in position by trip line. Its black fishing line "track" is fastened behind top of column, threaded through thin black wire loop from top of bat's body, and is tied off offstage above and beyond French windows.

When trip line releases bat on cue, its *pulling* fish line, attached to front of bat's body, is rapidly reeled in by crew member, again with large deep sea fishing reel, from his perch on A-ladder backstage of set's balcony.

GREEN LIGHT SUFFUSES MINA

A follow spotlight from front light booth is needed for this. Iris in to a "pin spot" *on Mina's face only* so that the mysterious light will not spill onto other characters near her during the scene.

COUNT DRACULA APPEARS THROUGH
SCRIM PAINTING OVER MANTEL

See set diagram. This is basically a simple stage trick but always effective. As suggested in directions within the scene itself, stage lights dim down as *lights behind scrim painting come up* on Count Dracula, standing on platform behind painting, making him visible through the portrait and within the portrait's frame.

When the hypnosis scene with Sybil is finished, lights behind the scrim dim out, stage lights brighten and Count Dracula seems to melt away as the painting again appears clearly. Dracula then descends backstage platform steps, goes to secret panel in UR wall, ready to enter in blackout to conceal himself behind sofa.

SYBIL BREAKS BATSWORT GARLAND, REMOVES IT FROM MINA'S NECK

The artificial flowers making up the Batswort garland are well secured by stout cord or heavy carpet thread *except* at one point. There the circlet of blossoms is held together by thin, easily broken string. Sybil breaks garland at this point, turning it into a long string of flowers which she slips from under the sleeping Mina's neck.

BAT FLIES THROUGH WINDOW AND OUT OVER AUDIENCE

This spectacular effect startles the audience. It is the trickiest to rig, but worth it. Depending on size and length of your auditorium and whether you have mezzanine or balcony, front light booth or side boxes for spectators—at any one of which bat's flight may end, the rigging suggested here will have to be adjusted to your theatre.

Should your stage's house curtain be the *drop type,* a note on special bat rigging follows these directions which are applicable, primarily, to the stage with front *traveler curtain.*

The 3rd prop Bat is pre-set backstage, just as his predecessors, above and beyond French windows and kept in position by trip line. His black fishing line "track," tied off backstage as were the others, goes through thin black wire loop from top of bat's body and the other end of track line has been *fastened before performance* to edge of mezzanine or front light booth, theatre box or wherever bat is to land. This means that track line stretches from stage and above audience through entire first two acts. So does the "pulling line," attached to front of bat's body backstage and stretching over auditorium to the large, deep sea fishing reel to be manipulated by crew member out front. Sharp-eyed spectators may spot these two fishing lines above them and conjecture as to their purpose, but the majority of the audience won't notice them since they are thin, black and high overhead.

As before, trip line releases bat on cue and crew member, crouched at mezzanine rail or in front light booth or theatre box seat, quickly reels bat forward through French windows, over the heads of the actors as they rush downstage in pursuit, then out over the audience. An additional scare for patrons is to have the track line suddenly slackened from backstage so that the bat swoops low, almost touching spectators' heads and then on up out of sight. Track line is then pulled semi-taut again from backstage and traveler curtains close around the track line in Act Two blackout.

If possible, during the blackout, crew man should detach bat from auditorium track line end and carry it backstage along with his reel. If this is not practical in your theatre, plan to have the bat end its flight in a small box with cloth flap front. This bat box is attached to mezzanine edge or wherever bat is to land. Crew man secures bat in box, then drops flap over its front so that audience will not see an inert prop bat hanging overhead for the rest of the evening.

During intermission #3 bat's *track line is detached backstage,* dropped and then slid along floor *under* front curtain to extreme Down Right.

Wind track line so that it will not tangle and hoist it *at Right edge* of front curtain to its former height. Then hang wound up track line *inside* Right proscenium *in front of house curtain.* This clears track line from overhead onstage so that black drapes or painted drop may be brought in for quick change to Crypt, Act Three—Scene 2, without breaking fishline.

SPECIAL RIGGING FOR STAGE WITH DROP FRONT CURTAIN INSTEAD OF FRONT TRAVELER
(Bat Over Audience, Continued:)

A *fourth* prop bat is needed here as are *two crew men and two deep sea fishing reels.*

Bat #3 flies only from beyond window to above actors onstage, then swoops up to disappear behind top of false inner proscenium. Bat is reeled in by crew man on specially constructed catwalk above false proscenium or from above stage in fly gallery.

Immediately after Bat #3 vanishes above false proscenium,

duplicate prop bat #4 is released *from behind edge of real* proscenium and is reeled over audience by crew man out front. Thus no bat track line is *between* real and false proscenium for curtain's descent.

ACT THREE
Scene One

JONATHAN'S T-SHIRT RIPPED TO SHREDS IN FIGHT SCENE
See Costume Plot.

LEFT STAIRWAY BOOKCASE SWINGS OPEN UPSTAGE
See set diagram. This effect is used twice in Scene 1, manually controlled by crew member backstage Left.

VERTICAL STRIP OF LIGHT MOVES ABOUT STAGE TO REPRESENT THE INVISIBLE COUNT DRACULA
The same follow spotlight from front booth is used as for the green pin spot on Mina. In this instance, a "blind" is slipped in front of the lens to get the effect of a strip of light (rather than normal circular spot) to represent a man's height and width. Light strip is first focused at center of open French windows as the invisible Count "enters." As he is supposedly approaching desk and desk chair moves as though he'd pulled it out to sit, *iris in to pin spot only* held on high back of chair when Dracula "sits" and chair moves back into regular position at desk. Otherwise, without using pin spot effect for this business, *strip* of light would spill across desk top and down desk front.

When Count Dracula "rises" and chair mysteriously moves away from desk again, pin spot moves to center, then becomes strip of light as he "sits" on sofa and center cushion sinks, etc. Maintain light strip as the unseen Count "rises," moves Right and mounts Right stairway to third step platform level. On cue, light strip fades out when Dracula is supposed to climb steps further and exit above to second floor.

If your auditorium is very large and normal follow spot proves inadequate for this effect, you may have to use a carbon-arc spotlight. Carbon-arc spots may be rented from theatrical supply houses or purchased. However, if your production budget prohibits such expense or should the use of any follow spotlight be impractical in your auditorium, this whole lighting effect may be eliminated. The uncanny movements of the desk chair, the sinking and rising of the sofa's seat cushion and Professor Van Helsing's remarks to the invisible Count Dracula clearly establish that he is supposed to be in the room.

DESK CHAIR MOVES UNAIDED

The high backed mahogany chair behind desk has its *Upstage Left* leg on a pivot through ground cloth and stage floor. Strong wires through screw eyes under ground cloth to backstage Left are attached to chair's *Upstage Right leg* and to *Downstage Left leg*. These wires, with wooden handles at their ends offstage, worked by a crew member backstage on cue create the effects of the invisible Count's moving chair, sitting etc.

Pulling wire attached to Upstage Right leg moves chair away from desk; pulling wire attached to Downstage Left leg returns chair to its usual place.

The chair's back should be gleaming with high polish to catch the light. Further, some sort of scroll work, simulated mother-of-pearl inlay, or brass studding on upper part of chair back facing the desk will help audience to see chair's movements.

For quick change to Scene 2, leg wires are slackened from backstage, chair is pivoted to face upstage where other furniture is stored in scene change, all concealed behind black curtain brought in or painted drop lowered as background for Crypt.

SINKING AND RISING OF MIDDLE SOFA SEAT CUSHION

This surprising effect both baffles and amuses the audience and evokes an audible murmur throughout the house at each performance. The sofa's center seat cushion is rigged to depress and then plump up again when the invisible Count Dracula "sits" and "rises." Sofa's slip cover, with flounce to the floor, and the three seat cushion covers must be of fairly *light colored material* to make cushion's action carry to whole audience. (Dark material defeats the purpose.)

Construction: Remove center cushion cover. Sew four small metal plates or metal rings to cushion's topside upholstery, about 3 to 4 inches in from each corner. Attach wires to the four plates or rings, run wires through cushion springs to *cen-*

ter of cushion's *underside*. Braid the four wire ends into one, replace cushion cover leaving braided wire protruding from underside.

Cut small hole through sofa body directly under middle cushion; run braided wire through this hole. Fit center cushion back into normal position. Attach braided wire to sturdy metal ring *beneath* sofa's center. Strong dog collar clasp-hook clips onto this ring under sofa and is fastened to length of wire leading through large screw eye in floor directly under sofa. This "pulling wire" then runs beneath ground cloth to backstage, going through other screw eyes in a straight line en route, with thin strips of wood *at each side of wire* forming a track for wire. This wooden track also protects both wire and screw eyes from actor's feet during performance.

The pulling wire terminates backstage Up Right (in general area behind fireplace) where it is fastened to a double-grip wooden handle. When stagehand pulls wire taut, center sofa seat cushion depresses on cue. Relaxing tension on wire makes cushion plump up again as the imperceptible Count supposedly rises from sitting position.

Following this action, wire is slackened from backstage so that, near end of Scene 1, sofa may be turned endwise toward audience to prove Dracula is not behind it after vanishing from inside his cape. To enable Jonathan and Dr. Seward to swing sofa around easily, sofa legs are on casters. Small wood blocks placed at two rear leg casters prevent sofa's moving out of position until, as Jonathan and Dr. Seward close in from each side to Count Dracula behind sofa, each of the two actors unobtrusively pushes a wood block aside with his foot, freeing two rear casters for half-circle shift of sofa.

For FAST SCENE CHANGE to Crypt, clasp-hook is detached from ring beneath sofa, sofa is moved upstage and concealed with other furniture behind black drapes or drop curtain brought in for Crypt background.

COUNT DRACULA VANISHES FROM CAPE
WITH STAGE LIGHTS UP FULL

See explanation within directions for the sence proper, just before curtain of Act Three, Scene 1. See also Costume Plot notes re. construction of cape.

ACT THREE

Scene Two

WOODEN STAKE DRIVEN THROUGH COUNT DRACULA'S HEART

Count Dracula's coffin, set on raised support on wheels to roll it onstage quickly, is a prop which must be built rather than a standard casket. It is without lid; the upper half of its downstage side is hinged to hang down so that Dracula is seen in profile from the waist up. *Beneath* bottom of coffin, on its upstage side, a box of sand is fastened to receive tip end and most of wooden stake as it is supposedly driven into the Count's heart.

As indicated in the scene's directions, Dr. Seward places stake in position which, from audience, appears to be over Count Dracula's heart. In actuality it is between Dracula's left arm and chest. While Dr. Seward holds and guides the stake, Professor Van Helsing drives it down with three measured blows of his heavy wooden mallet. The sand box below Dracula's left side will keep the stake upright, especially when the Count's arms shoot up from coffin in a vain attempt to reach Van Helsing and Seward, then fall lifelessly at coffin's sides.

PSYCHEDELIC LIGHTS FLASH OVER AUDIENCE WITH EACH STROKE OF THE MALLET

This effect, requiring special lights placed throughout the auditorium, can be omitted. It is theatrical, but optional.

Note: In view of the tricks, special effects, frequent light and sound cues, etc. requisite to the production, it is advisable to plan two or more full technical rehearsals *for the stage crew alone* without cast members. Thus any technical flaw can be righted well before the cast has its first technical run-through and, ultimately, dress rehearsals.

PROPERTY PLOT

ACT ONE

Full length sofa:
   1930's style, 3 seat cushions. Center cushion rigged
End table:
   Left of sofa. Ashtray, safety matches, etc. on table
Mahogany fire bench:
   Small, backless, U. S. R. below fireplace
Brass andirons
Grate of glowing coals (electric)
Brass foot rail   } In fireplace
Flash Pot:
   Loaded, concealed behind foot rail
Pair of heavy brass candlesticks:
   With tall dark candles, on fireplace mantel
High wooden stool with foot rungs:
   R. corner of fireplace. Stool must be reinforced. Renfield crashes it to floor in each performance
Old fashioned bell cord:
   Hanging above stool on wall R. of fireplace. Firmly attached to upper molding for Acts One and Two; rigged to come down with one tug in Act Three
Small, graceful, lightweight swivel chair:
   Not business office nor library type but a decorative swivel for the home. U. C. between sofa and desk. Frequently moved and must have well oiled, silent wheels
Flat top mahogany desk:
   L. C., drawers facing U. S. Black 1930's French cradle telephone, no dial, on L. end of desk. Low desk lamp on R. end. Electric push button fastened to U. S. R. corner of desk top. No offstage sound needed for buzzer. Silver cigarette box with cigarettes, short length, with practical silver lighter nearby on desk
Triangular shaped bar:
   Fits into or built into U. L. corner of room. Mahogany in appearance, highly polished. Bar has exposed upper and lower triangular shelves for English liquor bottles, Seltzer water bottle, cut glass sherry decanter with stopper, highball glasses,

130

wine glasses, etc., leaving surface of bar fairly free for coffee trays used in Acts Two and Three

High backed mahogany desk chair:
Above desk, rigged for magic effects in Act Three

Old fashioned leather tuffet or hassock:
D. L. below Left stairs. Lightweight enough for Jonathan to carry, for Hennessey to lift easily

Window draperies and *gauze curtains:*
Open at Rise

French Windows opened into room:
Door D. R.—closed

OFFSTAGE U. C.:
Prop Bat #1 pre-set:
For flight from backstage through French windows and to above column Right

OFF LEFT:
Expensive leather overnight suitcase:
Good sized and weighted

Matching leather briefcase:
Old style with leather straps, no zipper ⎫ for Jonathan

Gray plush jewelry box:
Inside briefcase, contains triple strand of pearls (Mina)

Thin, flat leather cigarette case:
With cigarettes and pocket lighter. (Jonathan, personal props)

Tray of canapes:
Two canapes are soft for Van Helsing to chew and swallow quickly for handshake bit with Jonathan

Leather suitcase and Gladstone bag:
Both ancient and battered, both weighted. For Dr. Seward to bring onstage as Van Helsing's luggage

Trick, prepared cigarette:
For magic flaming cigarette business, with abrasive paper for palm and masking tape. (Count Dracula)

OFF RIGHT:
Small ostrich feather folding fan:
(Sybil)

White linen handkerchief:
Folded for Tuxedo breast pocket. (Jonathan, personal prop)

Small set of dinner chimes:
  On polished wood frame. Felt-wrapped mallet for striking
  chimes. (Hennessey)
Chiffon neck scarf:
  Light pastel shade to complement Mina's gown
Vampire fangs:
  For Count Dracula. (Personal prop)
Large, deep sea fishing reel and *high A-ladder:*
  For crew member to reel in flying Bat

ACT TWO

STRIKE:
Canape tray from desk
Mina's chiffon scarf from floor to:
  Off Right prop table for Count Dracula
SET:
Clean ashtrays
Tuffet:
  Return to original position below Left stairs
Fire bench:
  Return to below fireplace
One empty tray:
  On bar for Wesley
Flash Pot reloaded
English candy box:
  Half full of small, assorted soft chocolates. Box with lid
  closed is on desk, just left of telephone cradle-base
3 partially filled highball glasses:
  One each on desk, end table and mantel
Check cigarettes and lighter:
  On desk
Window draperies and *gauze curtains:*
  Closed at Rise
Door D. R.:
  Closed
OFF LEFT:
Van Helsing's Gladstone Bag:
  For Jonathan

Good sized cardboard carton:
Plain, without advertising lettering.
Carton is wrapped with brown paper,
tied with heavy twine. Carton is
weighted aside from the following
props it contains:

> *4 small crucifixes* of shining metal
> to catch light, about 5 inches high to
> fit into men's breast pockets without
> showing over pocket top
> Only one of 4 crucifixes is on a
> chain (for Mina)
> *Sprays* of *"Batswort"* blossoms,
> small artificial flowers with soft
> cloth petals of white and light blue.
> *Garland* of Batswort flowers and
> leaves to go round Mina's neck

for
Van Helsing

Small pocket penknife:
Van Helsing, personal prop

Copy of London Times:
Folded to fit into Van Helsing's jacket side pocket with part
of newspaper protruding. If edition is too thick remove inner
pages

Small oval shaped boudoir mirror:
About 12" high so as not to shield Mina's face from audience.
Mirror is pier glass type, on its own stand with upright sup-
ports at either side. Frame is on pivots so it can be tilted.
Use thin, inexpensive sheet glass cut oval shaped. Mirror is
blackened or silvered on back; audience never sees front
surface

OFF RIGHT:

Prop Bat #2 pre-set:
Behind top of Right column for flight through French windows and up out of sight offstage

Door key:
With easily identifiable red tag attached (Wesley)

Personal Props for Count Dracula:
Duplicate key with red tag in white vest pocket
Shining gold locket on slender gold chain, tucked in white
vest pocket

Vampire fangs
Magician's apparatus ("Silk Appearer") with Mina's *chiffon scarf* from Act One
Magician's apparatus (Cigarette Vanisher")
2nd trick, prepared cigarette for flaming effect repeated
Abrasive paper and masking tape for palm of left hand
Long handled, silver backed hairbrush:
    For Mina
Coffee tray:
    With china coffee pot, coffee, 3 cups and saucers, teaspoons, sugar, cream
OFFSTAGE UP CENTER:
Prop Bat #3 pre-set:
    For flight in through French windows, down stage center, then swoop low over audience heads and disappear at back of auditorium
Large, deep sea fishing reel and *high A-ladder:*
    For crew member to reel in flying Bat #2 from Right column out through windows
AT BACK OF AUDITORIUM:
Large, deep sea fishing reel:
    For crew member to reel in flying Bat #3 out over audience

ACT THREE
Scene One

STRIKE:
Tray of used glasses:
    From bar; left by Wesley
Coffee tray:
    With china coffee pot, etc. from bar
London Times:
    From desk
Mina's hairbrush:
    From desk
SET:
Tuffet:
    To D. L. C. below desk, on level with D. S. side of Left staircase
Oval boudoir mirror:
    Fastened to desk top, mirror's pivots tightened so it won't spin when glass is smashed by Count Dracula

Bell cord:
  To come down with one quick tug
Pipe, pocket sized tobacco pouch, matches:
  On end table Left of sofa (Van Helsing)
Small pistol loaded with blanks:
  Ready on desk for Jonathan to hold at Rise
2nd pistol loaded with blanks:
  Held ready offstage by Stage Manager near French windows
  should Jonathan's pistol fail
Desk drawer keys:
  On desk for Dr. Seward to pocket at "Places" call
Sharp pointed wooden stake:
  18″ long, 2½″ in circumference on desk
Heavy wooden mallet:
  With metal striking tips, on desk beside stake
Cut glass sherry decanter with stopper:
  Now half full, on bar
Coffee tray:
  With coffee pot, cold coffee, cups, saucers, etc. on bar. These
  props are different from those used in Act Two
Jonathan's jacket and necktie:
  Laid over sofa back, Right end. Check: *Crucifix* in jacket's
  outer breast pocket
Check cigarettes and lighter:
  On desk
Window draperies and *curtains:*
  Open at Rise
French windows:
  Opened out onto balcony
Door D. R. closed

OFF LEFT:
Glass phial with stopper:
  Phial contains water. Must be the right size to fit into Van
  Helsing's inner breast pocket
Duplicate "Batswort" garland:
  Same as garland Mina wears earlier in Scene 1 except it is
  weighted for Van Helsing to toss across the stage to Seward.
  Mina carries this weighted garland on her reentry when
  wearing the voluptuous evening gown
Vampire fangs:
  For Mina

19th Century dress sword with good-sized cross bar handle.
(No guard!) for Jonathan

Duplicate cut glass sherry decanter:
Empty for Sybil's return from dining room. Or it can be the
same prop she carried from bar, drained offstage

OFF RIGHT:

Evening gown of dazzling color:
Folded for Mina to carry over her arm so little of the gown's
design is apparent

Small wicker sewing basket:
Should be lap-sized with wicker top on hinges. Contains
dozen or more spools of vari-colored thread, one matching
Mina's gown, sewing scissors, velvet pincushion, etc. (Sybil)

Silver coffee tray:
With silver coffee service, 3 fine china cups, saucers, etc.
(Hennessey)

"Batswort" garland and crucifix on chain:
For Mina (Personal props)

ACT THREE
Scene Two

STRIKE:

All furniture and onstage props:
Moved u. s. above line of black drapes or painted drop
brought in for Crypt background. (See "Special Effects" for
directions to free sofa from rigged cushion "pulling wire"
and how to pivot desk chair with its wires still attached)

Rugs:
Below sofa and desk, rolled and stored u. s.

SET:

Count Dracula's coffin:
Rolled in on wheeled base from off Left where Left wall
swings back. Wheels are then wood-blocked to prevent any
movement: *Check* box of sand below bottom of coffin

OFF LEFT:

Vampire fangs:
For Mina. (Personal prop)

Two practical flashlights:
For Jonathan and Seward. *Check* batteries, bulbs before each
performance

Wooden stake and mallet:
Van Helsing (Personal props) Retained from Scene 1

COSTUME PLOT
(*In order of each character's appearance in each act.*)

ACT ONE

SYBIL:

Sybil's clothes are costly disasters. Each ensemble is too girlish for a woman of her ample figure and evident middle-age. She's pushing fifty, but ignores it. Unaware that she's overripe, she dresses like an ingenue.

In Act One she appears in an evening gown of the 1930's. It is high fashion of the time, excellent material and expensive, but on Sybil it emphasizes what it should disguise. Her graying hair is fussily marcelled, her French heels too high for common sense and the bifocal glasses, bouncing from her bosom from an ornate chain, do not help. Coiffure, gown and satin slippers each tell us money has been spent—but in vain.

HENNESSEY:

Wears typical hospital or asylum attendant's jacket of pale gray or blue, anything but white which catches light. White shirt, necktie of unremarkable pattern and color, dark trousers, black hose and black shoes.

DR. SEWARD:

In tuxedo with the wide lapels of the 1930's. Dress shirt with wing collar, black bow tie, black silk socks and black patent leather pumps.

RENFIELD:

Standard asylum inmate's attire: light gray, almost colorless, slightly soiled denim trousers and jacket. Pale blue shirt open at the collar, no necktie, scuffed brown or black shoes with full rubber soles and heels for his stealthy movement.

WESLEY:

Duplicate of Hennessey's costume except the necktie is brighter and a bit daring.

JONATHAN:

Well fitted young businessman's suit of the period, shaped in at the waist, padded at the shoulders. The handkerchief in his breast pocket has three impeccable points and a small flower brightens his left lapel. Gleaming white shirt, expensive silk tie and a sparkling shine on his costly shoes all bespeak the successful young executive of the day.

Changes into tuxedo, dress shirt with wing collar, black tie, black silk socks and patent leather shoes.

MINA:

Her evening dress is of chiffon of flattering color, as low cut as fashion and mores of the '30's dared permit. Its lines are flowing and utterly feminine. High heeled silk evening shoes match her dress, her earrings are tasteful and simple, and at her neck she wears an old fashioned cameo on a wide velvet "choker" which is the same color as her gown and conceals the lower part of her throat. This choker is an important prop throughout Act One. Must have snaps at the back which Count Dracula can open easily to remove choker from Mina's throat.

COUNT DRACULA:

He is immaculately attired in white tie and tails, white vest, black silk hose and black patent leather pumps. On his first entrance he carries his silk opera hat and white kid evening gloves.

Over his shoulders he wears an evening cape of costly black satin lined with vibrant red silk and with a stiff, high standing collar which frames his head. The cape's red lining is webbed with fine black piping criss-crossing itself, like the veins of a bat's wings.

At each front edge of the cape there are finger-loops through which Count Dracula slips the little finger and ring finger of each hand, enabling him to hold the cape stretched open wide to make him, at such moments, resemble a gigantic bat. The finger-loops prevent his having to clutch edges of cape when he spreads its awesome fullness, leaving his hands free for stage business. The cape is never removed except for Act Three when he wears the trick cape described later in Costume Plot.

HEINRICH VAN HELSING:

His clothes are always rumpled. His suit is clean, but has a slept-in look. It is simply the garment of a middle-aged professional man with a busy life whose busy mind has neither time nor patience to dawdle over neat appearance. His shirt collars curl up at the tips, his tie is forever askew and his shoes would welcome a shine. Care must be observed that his wardrobe in no way suggests the derelict; rather that he never gives it a thought. His suit pockets bulge like fat woolen cheeks. They are sanctuaries for pipes, tobacco pouches, matches, pencil stubs, eyeglass cases and forgotten what-nots crammed into them some equally forgotten yesterday.

ACT TWO

JONATHAN:
Another business suit, dignified tie and shirt. Dark socks, black or cordovan shoes.

SYBIL:
Another ill chosen evening gown with evening shoes to match. She wears a long silk scarf of contrasting color over her shoulders, so long that occasionally it droops down behind her and she sits on it.

DR. SEWARD:
Subdued but tweedy English sports jacket, dark trousers, dark colored necktie, white shirt, black or oxblood shoes.

HENNESSEY:
Same costume as in Act One with different shirt and tie.

WESLEY:
Same costume as in Act One with change of shirt and tie.

COUNT DRACULA:
Same full dress suit and cape as in Act One but without silk top hat and kid gloves.

RENFIELD:
Same costume as in Act One.

VAN HELSING:
A different suit from Act One outfit, but just as rumpled with that built-in slept-in look.

MINA:
Wears a beautiful, soft colored, floor length silk nightgown, low cut so that it is almost (but not quite) revealing. Over it she wears a long, flowing negligee which trails slightly behind her. It is a negligee of considerable grace—but no warmth whatever. Satin bedroom slippers of pastel shade complement the ensemble. Her abundant hair hangs loose down her back.

ACT THREE

Scene One

JONATHAN:

Same suit as in Act Two with a change to pale blue or beige shirt. Shirt is open at the collar and the sleeves are rolled up to his elbows. Under his shirt he wears a T-shirt of thin material which will tear easily. Tiny nicks made with a razor blade and pre-cut in this T-shirt will facilitate Renfield's shredding it in the fight scene.

Jonathan's suit jacket and tie are across sofa back at Rise.
> *Note:* It is important that he, Dr. Seward and Van Helsing *all wear the same clothes as in Act Two* so that the audience can assume, but not know for certain, that the three crucifixes are still in their three jackets' breast pockets.

VAN HELSING:

Same costume as in Act Two with different necktie.

DR. SEWARD:

Same costume as in Act Two with different shirt and necktie. His tie is loosened but still knotted, and his shirt collar is open.

HENNESSEY:

Cotton pajamas of neutral color and lightweight robe tied with robe belt. He wears socks and shoes, the latter for fast footwork in fight with Renfield.

MINA:

Same or second nightgown, worn with same negligee as in Act Two. Her hair is piled high and she wears hose with evening shoes which will suit the evening gown into which she changes later. Round her neck are a garland of Batswort flowers and the small crucifix on its chain.

Halfway through Scene 1 Mina changes, not only her attire, but her whole personality. She appears in a brilliantly colored evening gown with its neckline lowered to a provocative level. It is backless, skin tight and designed for a voluptuary.

SYBIL:

Wears a fussy, embroidered, floor length nightgown with

high neck and baby ribbon bows on the bodice. Her silk or satin house robe is full enough to conceal the sherry decanter in its folds. She wears noisy bedroom slippers (mules) with clattering heels and pompons. Her hair has been tortured into old fashioned paper curlers and, as ever, the bifocals bounce from the bosom.

RENFIELD:

The usual drab, colorless institutional pajamas and a thin cotton robe which is open, flapping and beltless. He is barefoot.

WESLEY:

Pajamas, bathrobe with cord, similar to Hennessey's night attire but more colorful. He wears bedroom slippers, no socks, and his hair is tousled as though he'd just been roused from sleep.

COUNT DRACULA:

White tie and full dress suit as before, but with a different cape specially constructed for the escape scene. (See directions within the scene proper, just before the end of Scene 1.)

This cape is made on the general lines of the other and is also floor length, but is completely black without colored lining. Bottom hem weighted to prevent cape's flapping up during the "struggle scene" before Dracula disappears. Sewn into the cape and covered with black cloth is a light wire frame to hold the shape of Count Dracula's shoulders. Cape has black hood attached which is worn hanging down over back of his shoulders until the escape scene when he pulls the hood over his head. The hood *also* has a light wire frame within it to retain the outline of the back of Dracula's head when, once he's got away through the secret panel, both Jonathan and Seward hold the cape by wire framed shoulders and wire framed hood, making it appear Dracula is still in it. Then they realize it is empty, let cape sag and audience sees that Count Dracula has vanished.

ACT THREE
Scene Two

COUNT DRACULA:

Lies in his coffin dressed as in Scene 1, but *without* cape.

MINA:

Still in evening gown as in latter half of Scene 1.

JONATHAN:
Has donned his suit jacket over torn T-shirt; otherwise dressed as in Scene 1.

DR. SEWARD *and* VAN HELSING:
Same costumes as at the end of Scene 1.

DESCRIPTION OF CHARACTERS

HENNESSEY:
  In his early 30's, chief attendant at Dr. Seward's asylum. He is earnest, trim, hard working and pleasant. Must be physically strong to help subdue Renfield's violent derangement.

SYBIL SEWARD:
  Is somewhere in her late 40's, but won't say where. She's Dr. Seward's spinster sister, addle-pated, occasionally detached from reality and harmlessly touched in the head. Though she tipples sherry she is *never* the least intoxicated. Only late in Act Three does she give vent to two hiccups—both ladylike.
  Her choice of clothes is unfortunate. Everything she wears is fussy and frilly and stresses her ample, middle-aged figure. She is mistress of the non sequitur, unconsciously funny and a bit pathetic, but not played for pathos. In sum, Sybil is a slightly daft, cheerful romantic who's never known romance.

DR. ARTHUR SEWARD:
  A dignified, kindly, compassionate man in his mid-50's. He is frequently exasperated by (but affectionately patient with) the wandering vagaries of his sister's muddled mind. Essentially serious and straightforward, he is capable of quiet, unexpected humor.

RENFIELD:
  Is a schizophrenic inmate of indeterminate age, small stature and cadaverous complexion. He can be in his late 20's to early 30's, but must be supple and strong for the exertion and simulated violence required of the actor. His slight build makes his hidden strength all the more surprising to the audience.
  A true schizophrenic, he vacillates instantly from lunatic ravings to perfectly rational conversation. His hair is mussed, he is unshaven and he is given to quick, nervous movement. He has a strange slithering, gliding gait. There is something about him which suggests a snake.

WESLEY:
  Another asylum attendant, younger than Hennessey, a pleas-

ant nature, an easy smile, a little brash—but never rude. He, too, needs to be fairly strong to help control Renfield.

JONATHAN HARKER:

In his late 20's; at most early 30's. He is a likable, outgoing, well heeled, well dressed, successful architect. He must have considerable physical strength, especially for the fight scene with Renfield. Granted the fight is staged; nonetheless it is of taxing duration and demands the vigor of youth. Since in the fight Jonathan's shirt is off, his T-shirt is shredded and he is all but stripped to the waist, the actor should have an excellent physique.

MINA:

(Pronounced MEE-na; contraction of Wilhelmina.) Despite her illness and pallor, Mina Murray is a most attractive young woman in her early or mid-20's. She is beautifully dressed in a 1930's long flowing chiffon evening gown of striking hue. Her abundant hair is piled high in one of the more flattering styles of the time.

She is a gentle, warm-hearted girl, quick to respond to others' needs, but her strange malady has made her listless, inattentive and oddly remote. Her nerves are on edge, but she does her best to hide this—particularly from Jonathan. During the play, as she falls further under Count Dracula's supernatural power, her personality slowly changes to that of a seductive, scheming wanton. Before our eyes, she is turning into a Vampire.

COUNT DRACULA:

His age is hard to determine for reasons which become apparent in Act Three. He seems, perhaps, a distinguished 40. His countenance is arresting, lupine, cruel and coldly handsome. Though he is evil incarnate, he must have an appeal—be it physical or hypnotic—for the women in the play and the women in the audience. His humor is sardonic and Satan inspired. His manner is one of mockery; yet he can entice and captivate. His accent is slightly Continental, but not so authentically European as to lose clarity. When he speaks his voice not only insinuates but threatens.

HEINRICH VAN HELSING:

In his 50's, a few years older than Dr. Seward. He is a dedicated scientist and a genial man except when crossed over an issue he deems important. Then geniality is replaced by sternness. Normally he looks on his fellow man with a humorous eye.

Though rumpled in appearance and comfortable as an old shoe, he must be played with dignity. Van Helsing is the play's *spine*, the man who brings about its denouement. He is a character to whom audiences immediately respond and take to their hearts and the actor must avoid the danger of *overplaying it* "to the crowd." If he falls into that actor trap, the whole play is thrown off balance.

It is wise not to attempt a Dutch accent. Van Helsing's lines are too important in furthering the plot to be blurred by unfamiliar cadences of speech.

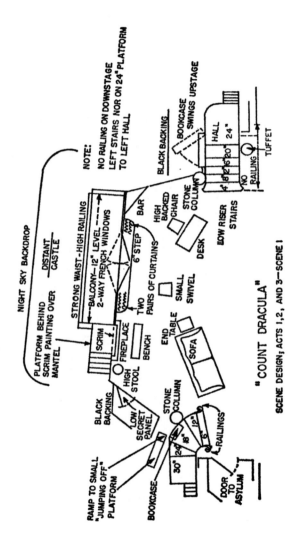

"COUNT DRACULA"

SCENE DESIGN; ACTS 1,2, AND 3—SCENE I

DESIGN BY PETER HARRIS

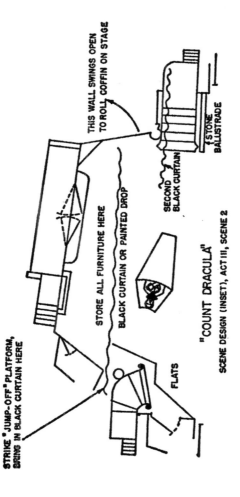

NOTE: SEE "SPECIAL EFFECTS" SECTION RE. QUICK CHANGE

THIS WALL SWINGS OPEN TO ROLL COFFIN ON STAGE

STONE BALUSTRADE

SECOND BLACK CURTAIN

STRIKE "JUMP-OFF" PLATFORM, BRING IN BLACK CURTAIN HERE

STORE ALL FURNITURE HERE

BLACK CURTAIN OR PAINTED DROP

FLATS

"COUNT DRACULA"
SCENE DESIGN (INSET), ACT III, SCENE 2

DESIGN BY PETER HARRIS

147

Count Dracula
**The saga of how Ted Tiller's script was born! ...
(edited, aided and abetted by Peter Harris!)**

The Time: Late 1971. *The Place*: A well-established Pro. Rep. Co. in West Springfield, MA ... which had on contract nine actors set to do the *original* "Dracula." Ten days before rehearsals they were denied the rights because the play had been optioned for a Broadway revival! The company management panicked (two weeks salary due those actors: *Disaster!*)

Their stage manager, William Guild, recalled that Ted Tiller and Peter Harris, both in a stock company years before (run by Guild's parents) had once saved the day with a quick rewrite of an old script! Quick call to them in NYC! The Bram Stoker novel "Dracula" was now in *public domain*, so why not a *new* script on the *mad* vampire, *drawn strictly from the novel*?!? Tiller & Harris to the rescue: no sleep for six days and nights; pages ripped from the typewriter and hastened to Massachusetts! Tiller at the typewriter; Harris glued to the *novel*; each seeing that nothing was used that was exclusively from the original *play* (or possibly from any film version)! Characters in the original *play* script which were *not* in the old novel could *not* be used! (There were at least two such roles in the original script ... both essential to the plot!) So on top of the frantic writing assignment, *new* characters had to be created to give those two "unknown" actors the employment due them!

Add to the chaos: Ted was a standby in the B'way revival of "No, No Nanette," in the role of

Ruby Keeler's husband, and Peter had taken on a new career as a salaried staff member of *Actor's Equity*! Yet we survived the challenge and added to the back of the script set ground plans, costume and property plots, detailed descriptions of "magic tricks" (special effects vital to the play) *and* a description of each character!

By a miracle it all got done and the Rep. Co. had its very own "*Count* Dracula," so named to distinguish it from the original play. And then a greater miracle! The B'way revival opened, an instant rave-success! And there was world-wide Samuel French, Inc. with their traditional "Dracula" tied up on B'way! Result: a contract to publish "Count Dracula." Tiller had offered Harris a by-line on the script for hanging in there during the birth pangs! Alas, Equity's legal advisors warned Harris that his job as a business "Rep", now full time, might be construed as a conflict of interest! So, Harris bowed off the front cover and settled for credit on the final two pages of set sketches.

The "Count" is now into its twelfth printing, with performances in every conceivable nation! Yet stranger-than-fiction *fate* keeps rearing its head: faithful friend Ted Tiller died in 1988 and willed half of the play royalties to Harris and half to his widowed sister-in-law. Keep ever in mind that in this mad, marvelous show-biz world, anything can happen - and what at first seems misfortune may tomorrow be the means of paying your rent!

ON WITH THE SHOW!

Peter Harris
July, 1997